Courtney has made a decision.

Her mother got out of the car and headed for the small door leading into the kitchen. "I just hope you know what you are doing, honey."

"I do, Mom. I do. I know God is behind this search. I've never been more sure of anything in my life. And just this afternoon, while sitting out at Aunt Agnes's, I realized what I must do next."

"What is that, dear?"

"I'm going to Illinois, to the small town where I was born. Surely I can find someone who knows something there."

Her mother looked almost shocked. "You don't mean it."

"Yes, I do."

BIRDIE L. ETCHISON lives in Washington State and knows much about the Willamette Valley, the setting for the majority of her books. She loves to research the colorful history of the United States and uses her research along with family stories to create wonderful novels.

Books by Birdie L. Etchison

HEARTSONG PRESENTS
HP123—The Heart Has Its Reasons
HP168—Love Shall Come Again
HP208—Love's Tender Path
HP252—Anna's Hope
HP272—Albert's Destiny
HP326—A Tender Melody

Don't miss out on any of our super romances. Write to us at the following address for information on our newest releases and club information.

Heartsong Presents Readers' Service
PO Box 719
Uhrichsville, OH 44683

Finding Courtney

Birdie L. Etchison

Heartsong Presents

With love and thanks to my Round Robin friends: Colleen, Elsie, Gail, Lauraine, Marcia, Marion, Pat, Ruby, Sandy, Woodeene.

A note from the author:

I love to hear from my readers! You may correspond with me by writing:

Birdie L. Etchison
Author Relations
PO Box 719
Uhrichsville, OH 44683

ISBN 1-57748-698-6

FINDING COURTNEY

Cover illustration by Adam Wallenta.

one

Courtney Adams was late. She hurried into the choir room and grabbed her robe.

"Hey, what's up?" her best friend, Tina, asked, turning to give her a hug. "Thought you were sick or something."

"Listen, we need to get together sometime. Maybe after church?"

Tina smiled. "Sure. If I can talk Mike into waiting."

Courtney frowned. Of course. She was constantly forgetting that Tina was married now. They'd been close friends for so many years, sharing everything that happened in their lives. All that had changed drastically after Tina married a year ago.

The organist was playing the introit, and the choir sang as they came into the sanctuary. Courtney pulled the robe down over her skirt, adjusted the collar, and straightened her long, dark hair with her hand. She hoped she looked okay.

Harmonizing with the sopranos, she quickly got into place and walked on down the aisle. She caught a smile from her mother and a wink from another friend. Tina's husband beamed at his wife. As often happened, Courtney got a lump in her throat when she saw her best friend with her husband. They had such a wonderful relationship, and she couldn't help thinking and hoping and wondering if someday she might find that perfect someone, too.

As the music ended, the choir assembled on the chairs off

to the side of the pulpit. Courtney scanned the audience. She had a bird's-eye view and could spot a visitor in a second. Her gaze came to light on a young man with immense shoulders and a smile on his face. He sat in the second pew. Her breath caught. Funny, but he had looked up just as she saw him, and they stared at each other for a long moment. She looked away as Pastor Sam asked for a show of hands of visitors. Each Sunday morning he passed out bookmarks to visitors—crosses made by the Women's Guild.

A hand shot up, and Courtney looked at the stranger again. "And where are you from?" Pastor Sam asked.

"Right here in Portland," came the answer. Courtney's heart skipped a beat. *Silly,* she admonished herself. *You know how you really feel about dating, so stop looking. Stop thinking that it might be possible for you to find someone, to be happy. It will never be possible, not until you find your birth mother.*

The other newcomers were lost to Courtney, though she usually paid careful attention. She felt a finger poking her ribs, and she realized they were standing to sing the first anthem, "O, For a Thousand Tongues to Sing!"

She could have sung that in her sleep. She'd always been in a choir, starting out with the junior choir. She couldn't remember a time when she hadn't attended a church, a time when she hadn't trusted and believed in the Lord. She had accepted Him as her personal Savior at a young age—her mother, that is, her adoptive mother, Alice, had recorded it in her *Seven-Year Baby Book.* Nobody could have asked for a more wonderful parent. And her father, God rest his soul, had been there for her, attending her games, taking her to swim lessons, always her best and loudest cheering section. She had been devastated when he died of a sudden heart attack two years ago. And Alice had been bereft, but they'd turned to the church, as always, and been uplifted.

Courtney wasn't sure when it first hit her, but one day she railed at God about not being able to find her real mother. She'd made every effort, sending letters, getting help from the library and the Internet, but so far had come to a dead end. Why wouldn't God let her find her mother? Would it be like Tina said, that she might find her and discover she didn't want to be found?

Courtney found out that was sometimes the case when she talked to a counselor about it. "Some birth mothers have not told their families about their pregnancy or about giving their child up. A grown person suddenly appearing on their doorstep can put a strain on a marriage and the relationship with their other children."

"But I have a right to know," Courtney had replied. "I need information about my medical background." Tears formed in her eyes as she remembered the year she was fifteen and had to drop out of high school. Her symptoms had been so weird. She had been exhausted every hour of every day. She could hardly eat, had no appetite, and though she wasn't in pain, she was listless. Her throat was raw and her side was tingly.

"Mono," the doctor had said at first. The tests came back negative. Then the numbness started; there were more tests, and an MRI ruled out multiple sclerosis or a brain tumor, but no diagnosis had ever been made.

"We'll fight this," Alice had said. "You're strong. Healthy. I know God can heal you."

And she had gotten better. Not immediately; she suffered through six months of being weak and nauseated. Then the symptoms left as fast as they had appeared.

"But what if it happens again?" had been Courtney's question. "I need to know what my birth mother had, if this is something that was passed on to me."

Alice had been helpful and understanding when Courtney said she wanted to find her birth mother. "I think I would feel that way also, dear. But," and her mother had enfolded her in her arms, "I think Tina is right. Your real mother may not want to be found."

"And if that's so," Courtney had said as she flounced across the kitchen, "then I'll accept that. I won't bug her. Believe me; I know when I am not wanted."

"Your father and I have loved you from that first moment you were placed in our arms."

❧

"Are you daydreaming, asleep, or what?" Tina was yanking on her robe. It was prayer time.

"I was just thinking."

"That's obvious," Tina whispered behind the back of her hand.

Courtney glanced up to find the stranger gazing at her again. She trembled.

Who is that gorgeous hunk? Tina wrote on the margin of her bulletin.

"How should I know?" Courtney said.

"And what's he doing here?"

"Maybe he's my brother."

Someone kicked the back of her chair. Courtney looked straight ahead, stifling a giggle. Sitting next to Tina meant sharing notes and thoughts. They'd done that when they were younger, but now they were supposedly mature twenty-three-year-old women, a bit old for passing notes.

She looked up and the man smiled, then winked at her.

She felt the color flood her cheeks. She tore her eyes away, hoping nobody had noticed. She knew, however, that her mother would have; she was that perceptive, and there would be questions once they got home.

When the service was over, and after she removed her choir robe, Courtney took longer than usual to fix her hair. She brushed it high on each side and secured it with gold clasps. Tina was always bugging her about cutting her hair, but so far she liked it just fine this way. She could French-braid it, wear a George Washington ponytail, or wear a high one like she had when she was in grade school. If she felt extra young, she wore two ponytails.

"Are you coming or what?" Tina stood in the doorway, her short hair in place and an impatient look on her round face. "Sometimes you are slower than slow."

Grabbing her handbag, she joined Tina on the way down the back stairs to the fellowship hall. "I had to fix my hair again," she finally said.

Tina stopped and looked down at her friend. "You wouldn't have that problem if you'd just get it cut."

Courtney felt her insides bristle. "Did I say it was a problem? You said it; I didn't." The last thing Courtney wanted was to feel out of sorts today. Her mind kept going to the stranger and how he had smiled and nodded at the sermon, how his gaze kept meeting hers, how he'd actually winked. No, today felt good. Today she could put aside some of her concerns. Missing her father. Wondering, again, how to locate her birth mother. Why was it so difficult for her when others had found lost ones in a day, sometimes even hours?

Tina had said something. Courtney knew it by the exasperated look on her face, and she'd missed it because she'd been daydreaming.

"I repeat," Tina began again, "your mind isn't receiving messages this morning."

Courtney turned and hugged her friend. Tina had always been plump, but now with her advancing pregnancy, she had become a round butterball. "I'm so excited with the baby coming and all. Guess I got to thinking about how you must feel about now."

There were others on the steps going down, so the two girls paused and Tina glanced up. "I can't get used to the kicks. I think I have a soccer player in there."

As they entered the already-filled hall, the smell of coffee made Courtney's stomach growl. All she'd had that morning was a quick cup and a day-old doughnut from the bread box.

"Hey." Tina pulled her close, nodding at one corner. "Isn't that the new guy over there? You can't miss him; he's so tall."

Courtney's heart zigged, then zagged. Yes, it was him. She felt like she was back in her freshman year when she'd had her first real boyfriend and they'd attended all the football games. Rick. Funny. She hadn't thought of him for years until now. Perhaps it was the height.

"Knowing you, you'll be over introducing yourself—" Tina was interrupted when Mike appeared, took her hand, and pulled her toward the refreshment table.

"I'll talk to you later," Courtney said to her friend's retreating back. Of course, if Mike had his way, he'd have her out the door in nothing flat. The baseball playoffs were coming up, and Mike was a baseball fan.

"Hey, Court, did you sign up for next Saturday's soup kitchen?" Karen was at her elbow, clipboard with dangling pencil in hand. "I think I need just two more."

"Sure, Karen. Put me down. You can forge my name."

Courtney continued along. One thing for sure, the church needed a larger fellowship hall. She wondered if there wouldn't be talk about an expansion in the near future. Relocating was out of the question, as members of the administrative board had already vetoed that idea. But they had the parking lot, and the owners of the next two lots had offered to sell in the event the church voted on adding a recreation hall.

She found herself in the stranger's corner. Finally. Courtney had always been good with words—could talk her way out of a traffic ticket, had talked her English teacher into giving her an A- instead of a B+ on a test. That ability had put her on the high school debate team, and Parkrose had taken first place at state competition the first time ever. But suddenly she felt awkward as her eyes met the stranger's. How could she be tongue-tied now? He was the first to speak as he held out his hand and took hers. She immediately felt the warmth, the strength in his handshake.

"Hello. I'm Steven, Steven Spencer. And you are?"

She felt color rise to her cheeks. "Courtney. Adams."

He still held her hand, and she found herself liking it very much.

"Do you want some coffee?" He smiled, revealing two dimples. "I decided to wait until the line dwindled down."

"I'd love some, but you are the guest. I should be the one offering to get yours—" She was babbling and she never, ever babbled—not even when she was a baby.

"Nonsense. We'll both go get it. You lead the way."

Courtney wove through the crowd, nodding at this one, pausing to hug another. Steven almost ran into her once but stopped in time.

Finally they both had coffee—black—and a chocolate brownie each. "I was led to this church this morning," Steven said. "Just thought I'd tell you that."

She felt mesmerized by his intense look. "Led? And just how do you mean?" She had a picture of someone putting a collar around his neck and leading him down the street to the church with the loud bell. So many churches had stopped ringing the bells ten minutes before the service. She was glad Parkrose Community had not.

"A voice told me to come here."

He was joking. She knew it. Courtney was often gullible, but not this time. "And you want me to believe this." She took a deep sip of her coffee, burning her tongue.

His dark eyes flashed with humor. "No. I am serious. Honest. A voice told me it was time I found a church to attend on Sundays. The voice just happens to belong to my grandmother."

"Oh." Well, that explained it.

"The only problem being Grams has been gone for nine years now."

Courtney nearly choked on the brownie. He reached over and touched her shoulder. "Are you okay?"

"I don't believe in voices," Courtney said. "Only God's voice."

He grinned now. How many expressions could one face have? "Oh, I believe in God's voice, but sometimes He has people to send important messages. Do you not believe this?"

Courtney found it difficult at the moment to know what she believed. She glanced away and noticed the fellowship hall was clearing out. People usually mingled for just a few minutes before heading for home. Obviously Mike and Tina had left already.

"I suppose you need to go." He was talking again, not waiting for her answer, but she wanted to give him one.

"I believe God delivers His message to many people, and I must admit I've heard voices leading me, helping me make a decision." She smiled and felt herself relax.

"Say, would you like to get lunch somewhere?" He looked expectant. "And if not now, perhaps another time?"

The coffee was gone, and she turned to set the cup down. "I have a standing date for lunch after church with my aunt Agnes in Gresham, but thanks."

Karen came over with the clipboard. "I can't get anyone else to sign up. Know somebody else, Court? Someone I may not know of?"

Karen was as tall as Courtney was short. She held the clipboard out to Courtney to read, but her eyes were on Steven. "Hi." She smiled. "Karen Martin."

"Steven Spencer. And what's this for?"

"Our soup kitchen Saturday morning. We take turns serving. The young adults have it this coming week. The men's group serves one week, the guild another, and the youth group one."

"This Saturday?" Steven smiled. "Sure, I'll do it."

Before Courtney could suggest a name, Steven had grabbed the clipboard and penciled his name in. "Ten o'clock? No problem."

"You didn't have to do that, but it was nice of you," Courtney said after Karen left.

"It's time to get involved in the community—"

"Is that something else the voice said to you?"

He laughed. "No. Actually, it was my own voice saying it the minute Karen said she needed one more person."

"It's fun. You'll like the people. So many walks of life." She was rambling again, and she didn't want to ramble in front of a stranger. Yet Steven didn't seem like a stranger. In some ways she felt she had known him for a long time. Funny how some people affected you that way.

"Listen, I'd better let you get on with your visit. Gresham's a few miles out there. I'll see you on Saturday, if not before." He handed her a card and removed another from the inside of his suit coat pocket. "I need your phone number."

She took the card. "Steven R. Spencer, Computer Analyst." The office was located in the downtown area. Her heart skipped another beat. In fact, he was located just four blocks from the law office on Fifth and Market where she worked as a legal assistant.

"I have a card also." She dug into the side pocket of her purse. Bob, her boss, had had the cards made for her, insisting that everyone must have a business card these days.

"I'll call you."

She nodded and watched him until he disappeared back up the stairs. She hoped he might turn around and look, but he didn't.

Courtney helped clear the table and made her way into the kitchen, where her mother was washing cups.

"Are you almost ready, Mom? You know Aunt Agnes. She'll be waiting and wondering why we took so long."

Alice Adams smiled and placed the last cup in the drainer. "I'll get out of this apron and be with you in a jiffy. Oh, by the way, wasn't that the new young visitor I saw you talking to?"

Courtney's cheeks flushed for what seemed like the fifth

time that day. "Steven? Yeah, he's new, but you already know that."

"You certainly were attentive, or was it the other way around?"

"Oh, Mom. You know how I am." But this was different. She hadn't felt this way ever. Her mother would like nothing better than to see Courtney married. How she'd love looking forward to a grandchild. But Courtney couldn't let herself dream about marriage, a child. Not yet. There were things she had to know about herself first. Stones to uncover. Medical facts to be discovered. She loved her adoptive mother with all her heart, and she'd been even closer to her adopted father, but she had to know who she was. It was that simple. Janelle Landers was the name of her birth mother. And Janelle Landers must be found.

With sweaters slung over their arms, Courtney and her mom went up the steps and out into the golden sunshine of the Sunday afternoon.

two

Steven walked the three blocks to his beat-up Ford. It needed a paint job, but it still ran and got good gas mileage. The kid he had working for him—just hired—had a new souped-up Trans Am, but Steven didn't want the payments that came with a new car. He was happy with his old heap. He paused, struggling with the driver's door. It stuck, and he always had to use extra force. As he crawled in behind the wheel, he looked around for the first time in a long while. The interior was tacky. It never bothered him before, but now he imagined picking up Miss Courtney Adams and asking her to get into the rust bucket. Suddenly the Trans Am was looking good. Perhaps he could rent it from Jeff for a night.

The sun was more than beautiful today; it was gorgeous. As Steven drove west toward Portland downtown proper, his mind was filled with the hymns sung that morning, the preacher's message that seemed to speak right to him, and the smile from an angel who sang in the choir. An angel named Courtney. "Wow, Grams, when you hit me with something, you really hit me," he said aloud. "I hadn't realized how far I'd strayed from church or from meaningful things in my life."

Ordinarily he would have stopped by the deli on the corner, but he didn't feel like eating and didn't know what he'd order if he did. Surely he could find a crust of bread in the house, a bit of peanut butter, and enough coffee to make a pot. So he went straight home.

His apartment was small but adequate. The walls were bare, as if he'd just moved in yesterday, when in fact he'd moved to Portland over a year ago and had rented this apartment the first day. It was the only one he had looked at. It didn't matter if he had a view—way too costly—nor did he need a large living area. He never planned to entertain, anyway. A kitchen, bed, and closet were the basic needs.

He started a pot of coffee, then went to the bedroom and opened his closet. It had plenty of room inside. He owned one good suit, the dark one he'd worn today. Grams had told him when he bought one for high school graduation, "Buy black and you'll not be sorry. You can wear it for weddings and funerals, as well. Waste not, want not, Steven."

"Yeah, Grams, you taught me well. I find it difficult to buy another suit or a car. But not hard to let my heart be taken by a certain dark-haired girl with twinkling eyes."

He hung the suit jacket next to the three dress shirts: two white, plus the light blue he had almost worn. For some reason he had chosen the checked one and the aqua tie. He had thought they matched, but now as he looked in the bedroom mirror, he decided they did not. Maybe he was color-blind and hadn't realized it until this minute. Nobody had ever helped him be color-coordinated. He wore tan Dockers to work each morning and usually a favorite navy blue V-neck sweater, sometimes a red sweater, and on occasion a sweatshirt. Jeff had complained about the sweatshirt. "Not presenting a good image," he said.

When had he become so frugal? Suddenly he wished he had nicer threads, a new couch, and a few paintings on the wall. He changed into his Dockers and a sweater and went back to the kitchen.

The coffee was finished, but the bread had mold on it, so he threw it in the sink. This meant he'd have to go to the deli unless he ordered a pizza. Half now, half tomorrow. *Waste not, want not,* rang through his head again.

He flipped on the TV. Baseball, *Hercules,* a preacher pounding the pulpit, and an ice skating show. Not much on Sunday.

He eased into a chair and grabbed his day planner. He never thought he'd be one to plan his days, but he found it invaluable once he'd gotten the hang of it.

The week was busy, but next weekend was open. Clear. He jotted down the words, *Soup Kitchen, 9:30 A.M.* Courtney had said ten, but Steven always arrived early, allowing himself time for getting lost or finding a parking spot.

He closed the book and wondered what it would be like to work next to Courtney. Would he be handing over the rolls or ladling up soup? Maybe he'd be in the kitchen washing up things. That would be okay. Grams had taught him to cook—not that he did so anymore. She'd also taught him to wash dishes and vacuum floors. "Men need to know how to do all things in the house," she'd said. "You never know when your wife might be sick or have a baby or something."

"What if I don't get married?" he'd asked. He was ten then, a tall, skin-and-bones, freckle-faced kid. Somehow he could not ever imagine marrying, thinking people rated marriage far higher than it deserved.

"You'll find someone one day and you'll wonder how you could ever feel so wonderful inside. And when that day comes, you'll want to commit, but be patient, Steven. Patience is a virtue, as the Lord tells us in the Good Book."

Patience. Steven had been patient most of his life. It was always the other guy who got the girl. He'd loved once in college, but he had been too backward, or so his roommate said. "Man, you see someone you like, you gotta make a move, man. You can't expect them to be aggressive. Some are, but those you may not want."

"Choose a Christian girl, and you'll be blessed many times over." That had been Grams's advice a few hours before she'd died. It was as if she knew she had to give him all the advice she had inside her. And Steven had soaked up the words, filled his mind with her presence, remembering the crooked smile he loved and the feel of the leathery cheek—soft, yet wrinkled from years of work in the sun. She'd been a true farm wife, never wanting to leave the Redmond ranch but having to when she had become ill. She'd hated the year she lived in the central Oregon town of Bend, yearning for the wide open spaces and wishing she still had the energy to raise cattle.

He had cried that night—cried because he missed her so much and because he felt he could have done more to make her happy. He had been expected to take over the ranch when he got out of school, but he didn't want that kind of life—and because he hadn't taken over, Grams had had to leave her beloved ranch when she became ill. The city called to him and though Grams said she understood, he doubted that she really did.

Steven strode to the refrigerator to look inside once more as if something would miraculously appear on the shelf. Bare. Totally. He decided then and there to go grocery shopping. Big-time. He could suddenly taste Grams's pot roast with potatoes and carrots surrounding it and the dark gravy that bubbled in the little pot on the stove. He'd get greens for making salad, and flour, sugar, baking powder—all the ingredients for making biscuits.

As he walked the ten blocks to the nearest store, he wondered, *What is wrong with me? Why did I walk? Now I'll struggle with the bags getting back to the apartment.* But the sun was still out, and a slight breeze blew in from the Willamette River. Summer would soon be over and fall in its brilliant colors would grace the hills on the opposite side. He loved fall the best—always would.

The cashier flashed him a warm smile and asked, "How are you this afternoon?"

He nodded. "Fine, thanks," he responded. As he headed out the door with two bags filled to the brim, he wondered if she was just being friendly or if he could have asked her out and had her accept. Courtney's face crossed his mind again. He had to see her before Saturday. How could he possibly wait that long? He wondered if she liked baseball. There was a Portland Rockies game on Wednesday. He laughed as he remembered asking his last date if she would like to see a game.

"I'd be bored out of my tree," she had said. Did he dare ask Courtney? Yet, wouldn't it be time to discover what she liked now before he became more interested?

He unlocked the downstairs door and took the stairs to the third floor.

The food halfway filled his refrigerator and one cupboard. Satisfied, he made a tuna fish sandwich with a slab of cheese on top and sprouts on top of that. And lots of mayo.

Next he'd go to Lloyd Center Mall, to the tall men's shop, since he always needed extra long sleeves and length in everything. Had he ever been short? He couldn't remember a time. Even when he'd played Little League and later joined Babe Ruth, he'd been put out in the field because his long arms could catch the fly balls.

He turned on the rest of the ball game, though it was the Yankees playing Cleveland and he was a National League fan, mainly the Cardinals.

After finishing his sandwich, topped off by another cup of coffee, Steven left for his second shopping trip of the day.

And the Lord said on the seventh day ye shall rest rang through his mind as he headed for the Ford. *Rest. How does one rest? Does one spend the day in prayer? Reading the Bible? Attending the evening service? Bingo. Of course. They must have an evening service. Wasn't that when the youth groups met? And if youth groups met, wouldn't the young adults' group also meet?*

He found the bulletin in the front seat and looked at the back at the announcements. Evening service was at 6 P.M.

He would be there, but first things first.

Minutes later, Steven was in the mall and suddenly felt like a child in a toy store at Christmas. The men's store had never held such fascination for him. He bought two pairs of casual slacks, different colors than the usual tan (Jeff would be surprised), a couple of tees, and new socks. Invariably, he lost at least one when he washed clothes each week. Someday he'd run an investigation to see where lost socks went. There had to be a sock heaven somewhere. He also purchased a lightweight jacket and two dressy shirts, one a burgundy silk (Jeff really would think he'd taken leave of his senses), and a casual shirt with a button-down collar.

"Well, Grams, I hope you aren't turning over in your grave. I just spent $350 and didn't even buy a suit or a pair of shoes!" he muttered as he walked to his car.

This time the door of his old Ford annoyed him more than usual. He hit it twice before it opened. Maybe the time had come to consider buying a newer model—not brand new, but something more serviceable. He could hear Jeff's voice now. "A man of your means needs a better car, if you don't mind my saying so."

As Steven made his way west on Multnomah and across the Broadway Bridge, he felt good. Lighthearted. He had food. He had clothes. He had a girl. Well, maybe he had a girl. It was a bit early to get his hopes up.

After traveling the three flights, his arms loaded down for the second time that day, he filled the hangers in his closet and put the socks in the top drawer. The new clothes looked good.

He opened a soda and reached for the phone.

"Jeff, I know this is going to sound crazy, but can I rent your car for one evening?"

"What say you?" The TV blared in the background, and Jeff was chewing on potato chips or something equally loud. "Man, you want to rent my car? Are you okay, Steven?"

Steven laughed. "Yes. I just need something better than mine tonight; probably three hours tops."

"Man, I'm not heading out, so you can have it. Just be sure you don't park too close to anybody. People aren't too careful about opening their doors and dinging the one next to them."

"I know. I'll take care of your baby; never fear."

After jotting down the address, Steven made another sandwich, a fried egg this time with a dab of ketchup and a ton of butter. It was the only sandwich on which he didn't use mayo.

He flipped on the evening news, saw that it was disastrous as always, and flipped it right back off. He'd rather read than hear about someone shooting someone else. The forecast was for an overcast morning. He had always liked to know what the weather was going to be.

As Steven paced his apartment, not knowing why he was doing so, he surveyed the bare walls again. A Renoir print would go well on the one wall, and of course, a Monet. He should go to the galleries in town and select a local artist as well. Classics were great, but he liked to support Portlanders, too.

That would mean another shopping trip. Then he'd think about the car. This meant his checking account would dwindle, but he had his mutual funds and the stocks to fall back on. Business was doing fantastically well, so why not spend it? "You can't take it with you, Steven, but you need enough to live on. Spend wisely."

"Well, Grams," he sat back down in his favorite chair, putting his hands behind his head, "do you think I spent too much today?"

He showered for the second time that day, then decided to go casual for the evening service, wearing his new button-down shirt with his Dockers and the light jacket.

Steven thought about why he'd come to Portland. He had left Central Oregon, where he'd lived all his life and liked the weather better since it rained less, but decided to move to a larger city for his expanding business. Portland seemed about right. He'd give it two years, then if he didn't like it, he could move to Seattle or maybe even south to California. He now knew why God had led him to Portland and why Grams had made him realize he needed God in his life again. He needed to get involved in a church—meet good people. Well, he had, hadn't he? He'd found the right church on the first try.

Humming, he took the stairs rather than the elevator to the ground floor and to the garage where his car waited.

He pounded the door twice. "Sorry, ol' friend. You're going to sit over in front of Jeff's house for a bit. Man, are his neighbors going to wonder what happened to him." Smiling, Steven roared out of the underground garage and headed back across the river for the third time that day.

three

Courtney rolled the window down as they traveled east on Powell. She could have taken the freeway and her mother asked why she had not, since she liked to arrive at least by one.

"I just want to go the slower way today, if that's okay."

"Of course, darling. I'm just along for the ride, anyway."

Courtney reached over and squeezed her mother's hand. Aunt Agnes was Alice's older sister and had lived alone for the past five years. The sisters always reminisced about losing their husbands and about being widows, while Courtney usually sat and worked on a rug she was hooking.

"I do wish you'd come to live with me," her mother said to Agnes, as always, the minute they arrived. "You know how I dislike rattling around in that big old house."

"Then sell it and come live with me."

"In Gresham?"

Courtney smiled as she threaded blue yarn onto the large needle. She had the litany memorized. Neither sister wanted to move, though they loved each other dearly. Agnes had not had children either and had looked into adoption, but nothing ever came of it. Courtney had grown up without cousins since her father had been an only child. It was a lonely existence, though she'd never wanted for a thing. "God has His reasons for what happens," her mother always said. Courtney believed with all her heart in the goodness of God, in how He wanted only the best for her.

"Our girl has met a young man," her mother was saying now. Courtney looked up, her mouth falling open.

"What did you just say?"

Aunt Agnes smiled. "That you met a nice young man and—"

Courtney set the hook aside. "Mother's letting her imagination run wild. I only met Steven this morning."

"Mark my words; he'll be back for the evening service."

"Oh, sure. Right."

They had the usual lunch. Aunt Agnes liked tomato soup and grilled cheese sandwiches. For dessert there was a fruit plate, which in recent years included kiwi fruit and shortbread cookies. When the Girl Scouts had their cookie drive in March, Agnes bought two dozen boxes and put them in the freezer for use the rest of the year. There would be six cookies on the plate. Two apiece.

For some unexplainable reason, Courtney could only eat half a toasted cheese.

"But, dear heart, you always eat a whole sandwich with your cup of soup," her aunt protested.

"I told you she's in love."

"Mom!" Courtney felt like a small child with the two discussing her as if she weren't in the room. She never had liked that game.

"It's about time you thought about marriage," Aunt Agnes said, clearing the table of soup cups.

"I cannot yet and you know why, Auntie."

"Of course. But I don't think you're going to find your birth mother. If the good Lord wanted you to, you would have by now."

Courtney felt a stabbing sensation run through her. It could be true. Prayers were always answered but sometimes not in the way one had hoped.

They left at three. This never varied, either. Aunt Agnes had her nap at that time, and Courtney and her mother returned home to a house that seemed cold and empty now. Even when her father had been alive, only the two of them had gone to see Aunt Agnes. "That's for you women," he had said. "You three have such a good time visiting and having lunch. I'd just be in the way." They'd all gotten together for Thanksgiving and Christmas and for birthdays, but not Sundays.

"I wish I didn't believe what Agnes said, sweetie," Courtney's mother said as they headed back home, "but you must admit she has a point."

"I'm not giving up." Courtney knew there was an edge to her voice, but she couldn't help it. They'd discussed this endless times, and though Alice agreed that it was something Courtney should do, she couldn't help letting her doubts be known.

"What if you are thirty and you aren't any closer than you are now?"

"Is thirty the magic number now? I'll be an old maid if I'm not married at thirty?"

"Don't sound like that." Her mother's voice got choked up, but Courtney plunged on.

"Mother, I love you dearly, but you must let me do what I must."

"But the Internet search has shown nothing. Not even a trace."

Courtney pulled into the driveway and pointed the garage-door opener. The two-story Cape Cod was the sort of house she wanted someday, should she ever marry. It was roomy, yet had such a homey feel about it. It had the same white paint and green trim her father had painted it with two years ago, just before his heart attack. The south side where the hot afternoon sun hit was peeling in spots, but she doubted that they could ever paint over it.

"I know I should have had some news by now, but that doesn't mean I give it all up."

Her mother got out of the car and headed for the small door leading into the kitchen. "I just hope you know what you are doing, honey."

"I do, Mom. I do. I know God is behind this search. I've never been more sure of anything in my life. And just this afternoon, while sitting out at Aunt Agnes's, I realized what I must do next."

"What is that, dear?"

"I'm going to Illinois, to the small town where I was born. Surely I can find someone who knows something there."

Her mother looked almost shocked. "You don't mean it."

"Yes, I do."

"But what about work?"

"I have time coming. Remember, I didn't take the two weeks of vacation this year. Bob will let me go."

"Are you sure?"

"Mom, he owes me."

"Bob is also interested in you. Don't forget that."

Courtney groaned. Her mother was intuitive. Courtney had never mentioned that he'd asked her out. She liked her boss, but knew she couldn't like him in that way. He didn't know God, and what's more, he used people to his advantage. She could never, ever fall in love with a man like that.

"I'll be sure to give Bob plenty of notice."

"Oh, honey, maybe I should come with you."

"No. Mom." They were in the kitchen, and Courtney poured a cup of coffee and put it in the microwave. "I know that might be a good idea, but it's just something I must do myself."

"Are you sure you'll be all right?"

Her mother was frightened of several things, and her fears had become more apparent since her husband had died. She didn't like to be alone, nor did she like the dark. Courtney had suggested she get a dog, but she'd vetoed that idea. Courtney knew that she was thinking about being alone now and that the thought terrified her.

"You could go out to spend some time with Aunt Agnes. Why don't you plan on doing that?"

"Oh, honey, I don't want to impose."

"Impose? Your own sister?" Though Courtney had never had a sister, she'd often longed for one and wondered what it would have been like to have a sibling, someone to share her ups and downs with. That's why she and Tina had remained such good friends.

"I'll call Fran over at Country Travel first thing in the morning and see if they have any specials coming up."

"You're assuming Bob will let you off. . . ." Her mother's voice trailed off.

"If he doesn't, I quit."

"You wouldn't!"

"Watch me."

"Well, you have your inheritance from your father. That could hold you over for a while, but surely—"

"Mother, I know I won't get fired. What's more, if he did fire me, I know of another place where I could work. Don't worry needlessly. What did God say about the birds of the air? 'Look at the birds of the air; they do not sow or reap or store away in barns, and yet your heavenly Father feeds them. Are you not much more valuable than they?' Matthew 6:26."

"I know, I know. I never worried like this until your father died."

Courtney stopped, put her cup down, and drew her mother close. "I don't want you to be concerned about me. I'm old enough to take care of myself."

"A mother never stops being concerned about her children," Alice said through her tears. She looked out the window into the backyard. The grass was green, the trees were green, but she missed the flowers her husband had always planted. He had such a way with a garden, but the small plot where he grew cabbages and tomatoes was bare and brown. Bare and brown just like her heart.

four

Courtney and her mother arrived at church at five minutes to six. The piano played "Let a Little Sunshine In, Let a Little Sunshine In." Courtney hummed as she moved into one of the back pews. The view was better from the back, though her mother preferred the front. But Alice never moved because she liked sitting with Courtney, especially since she couldn't sit with her on Sunday morning when Courtney was in the choir.

"See? I told you." Her mother tugged at her arm. "He's here. That nice young man you talked to after church today."

Courtney's heart lurched. Could her mother be right? Should she be reading more into the depth of those pale blue eyes? She knew her face was flushed, so she touched her cheeks and willed the red to disappear.

"He's talking to Rod."

Rod was also single and had had an eye on Courtney since they were kids in junior high. Courtney thought of him as a brother and had told him so on more than one occasion.

"Look, dear. He's spotted you!"

"Mother," Courtney said under her breath. She felt like a small child on her way to the first day of school, with her mother hovering.

The three-member ensemble got on the stage and set up the sound equipment. This was Courtney's favorite part of the service. This and testimony time. The evening message was always short—ten minutes tops.

She glanced at the corner where the teenagers sat. They passed notes now, just as she and Tina had. Tina. Was Tina here tonight?

Courtney made a quick check, her eyes meeting Steven's. He waved, and the next thing she knew, he had left the pew and was making his way to her side of the church.

"That's one nice thing about him," her mother whispered her way. "He's on time. That's a true virtue; believe me."

Courtney squirmed. Of course her mother would say that. Courtney had struggled with being on time all her life. What would it be like to arrive early? She grinned at the thought.

He came down the other aisle and moved in next to Courtney. "I hope you don't mind if I sit here with you."

With no tie and what appeared to be a new denim jacket, he looked more casual. She liked the clean smell of him and moved to make room, when what she wanted to do was stay right there in that spot. Alice Adams leaned over, extending her hand. "So nice to have you attend evening service."

"Yes," Courtney added. "I didn't think I'd see you until Saturday."

He smiled and once more she was disarmed by the way his whole face looked, the eyes dancing, almost as if teasing her. "I go in for things in a big way. Once I'm committed, that is."

Suddenly Courtney realized she knew very little about him and wanted to know more. A sinking feeling hit as she knew she couldn't tell him much about herself.

The first song began, and Courtney's voice rang out. She

could feel Steven's eyes on her and she tried to hear his voice, but heard nothing but her mother's.

After the song, he nodded. "I'm glad I sat by you. Your voice warms my heart."

It was the second time she blushed that evening. *Why is he having this effect on me?* she wondered. *Nobody has ever made me feel like this.* She stared straight ahead, afraid to look in his direction, afraid of what she might do or not do. She'd probably forget where she was.

Testimony time was longer than usual, but Courtney didn't hear much. She clapped and smiled at the appropriate times. Then Steven stood.

"I've been looking for a church home," he said. "Been in the city for a year. I feel at home here and will definitely be back."

Cheers rose and hearty clapping filled the sanctuary. Evening service was always so informal. Courtney loved it, but her mother sometimes frowned. "Imagine playing 'Autumn Leaves' for service," she had humphed last week.

Steven sat and Courtney had a sudden impulse to reach over and take his hand, but common sense held her back. *Oh, Lord,* she prayed inwardly, *this man is going to mean a lot to me. I can tell. Give me a calm spirit. Please.*

After the service, they milled toward the door. "It's a nice night. Could I give you both a short ride to the ice cream store over on Division?"

Alice looked almost shocked. They'd never gone out for ice cream after the service.

"You two go on. I can drive the car home, Courtney."

"But I want you to come also, Mrs. Adams."

Alice looked flustered. "I—well, I don't know."

"Of course, Mom. C'mon. It'll be fun. It's a warm night,

and who wants to go home?"

"Why don't you take your car home and I'll follow?" Steven suggested.

The ice cream store buzzed with activity, but they found one booth in the front and sat. Courtney doubted she could eat. The two-mile ride over had been interesting. The car was nice, a Trans Am. She knew her mother was thinking that Steven must make good money. She'd hear all about it when they got home.

And then he spoke.

"Just want you to know this isn't my car. It's an employee's. He loaned it to me for the night."

"Oh," Courtney managed. But inside she wondered, *Why is he telling us this? Why would he feel the necessity to borrow a car? Is his own car a disaster?*

As if reading her mind, he went on. "My car, something I cannot seem to part with, has a problem with the doors. The passenger door refuses to open and the windows won't roll down."

Alice laughed. "Sounds like the car Courtney's father and I first owned."

Steven ordered pistachio nut ice cream, two scoops in one of the fancy dishes, and Courtney had her favorite chocolate/peanut butter, but Mrs. Adams ordered a waffle cone with vanilla.

"Vanilla? You sure, Mrs. Adams?" Steven stared at her in disbelief. "With all these flavors, you choose vanilla?"

She nodded. "It's my favorite, and they simply cannot improve on it."

Courtney wondered what she would put in her journal when she got home. *Tonight I had my first date with Steven, and Mom came along.*

On the way home they chatted about the community, why Portland was a good place to live, and how long the Adamses had lived in the suburb of Parkrose.

When Steven pulled into the driveway, Alice invited him in. He walked them to the door and stepped inside for a few minutes but didn't stay. "Tomorrow is going to be horrendous, as Mondays always are. Everyone who has had problems with their computer will have called in. Last week I had twelve calls on the machine."

"Oh, my, but that's a good problem to have, yes?" Alice remarked.

He nodded. "Yes, the business is doing well. I've also obtained a few accounts from large businesses in the downtown area, so that helps with expenses." He headed toward the door and Courtney followed.

Courtney walked down the sidewalk to his car in the driveway. The summer night was warm with a thousand stars beaming down on them. He took her hand impulsively.

She smiled, liking the warmth, the firmness of his large hand holding hers. "I love this time of day. It's almost magical."

"Yes." He stopped walking. "You know, your hair is beautiful with stardust in it."

"Why, thank you." Courtney used to feel embarrassed at compliments, but her mother told her, "All you do is thank the person. Works every time."

"Courtney, I don't know what is happening to me, but it's as if you're right in the middle of it and I need to know now—is there someone else?"

Wow, was all she could think. *One day, Lord. This is all happening in one day. How can that be? Is it right? Is it good?*

"There is no one right now," she finally said, her voice almost lost in the sounds of evening.

"I'm glad." He let her hand go. "I want to see you before Saturday. If you like baseball, I thought you might go to a Rockies game with me on Wednesday."

"I love baseball," she murmured. "I used to play when I was in grade school."

"Really? What position?"

"Catcher."

"That's the toughest position of all, if you ask me."

"Taking the gear on and off was the worst part."

"I played center," Steven said. He looked thoughtful. "I'm working on getting a men's softball team going, but we won't be playing until next year. Hey, I really must go. And thanks for going for ice cream."

Courtney watched as he dipped down low enough to get into the Trans Am. She tried to stifle her grin but couldn't. Steven waved and then he was gone. She stood in the glowing moonlight and looked at the sky. "Things have never happened this fast before, Lord, but I have to be careful," she whispered. "No way can I get serious with anyone until I know who brought me into the world. I just hope Steven understands that."

And with a deep sigh she moved toward the door of the Cape Cod.

five

Steven whistled all the way back across the river. He usually dreaded Mondays, but Monday meant he was that much closer to Tuesday, and Tuesday was next to Wednesday, and Wednesday night was the game. In the meantime, he'd concentrate on work and dream about things that might happen. *It's just too soon,* he kept thinking. *You can't fall for someone that quickly*. Yet hadn't he heard about love at first sight?

"That's your emotions speaking," Grams would have said. "You're letting your heart rule over your head and common sense."

He ran up the three flights and wasn't even panting when he got to 306.

The bare walls screamed out at him. Yeah. He had to go shopping for art—and soon. Maybe Courtney would like to accompany him. *Let's see.* He had the ball game Wednesday, soup kitchen on Saturday, and church Sunday. Saturday afternoon was free. A perfect time to browse through art galleries. He'd ask her at the game. And with that settled, he slipped into the recliner and dozed off while catching just half of the Major League baseball scores.

❧

Courtney floated into the house. Her mother was making noise in the kitchen. They really had not eaten much before church, and the ice cream only whetted her appetite.

"Mom?"

"I'm just fixing a little something. Come sit and talk to me."

Courtney pulled out a chair. The inquisition was about to begin. It had been this way when she'd dated Rod that one time. Then Lanny. And Rick. All just good friends, yet Alice always asked and always watched while Courtney talked, as if thinking this one could be the right one.

"I'm not asking any questions," Alice said as she placed a plate of crackers and peanut butter on the table.

"Now there's a switch," Courtney said, biting into a cracker.

"I don't need to, dear."

Courtney turned and stared. "Don't *need* to?"

"I have my ways of knowing. God gives me a nudge when I'm right, and I have this feeling about this young man. So polite and caring."

"Don't forget good looks, Mom. Looks are so important to you."

"I never said that."

"Didn't have to."

Grabbing a plain cracker, Courtney held it in her mouth a long while. She'd never forgotten the experiment in eighth-grade science. She could hear Mr. Arnold's voice now. "If you hold a saltine in your mouth for several minutes, the salt changes to sugar."

"What are you doing?" Alice asked.

"Eating a cracker."

"You're not listening to me."

"I can't get serious; you know that."

"Oh, dear. Not that. Please don't say this. It upsets me so much." Alice jumped up from the table and put a teakettle on.

"If you drink tea, you'll be up all night. You always complain the next morning."

Her mother nodded. "I know, but tea is soothing. It relaxes me."

"So one negative and one positive and the positive wins out. Good for you, Mom." Courtney pushed her chair back.

"Are you going to sit with me for a bit?"

Courtney pulled the chair back to the table. "Sure. For a bit. Tomorrow is a workday for me, though. Bob will not be in a good mood."

Alice stirred a scant teaspoon of sugar into her tea and held the cup up under her nose. It was apple cinnamon, her favorite.

"I just want to discuss this search thing."

Courtney sighed. "Mom, we've been over it before. You know how I feel and you just have to accept that."

This time she did leave the table, glancing back once at her mother leaning over, trying to hold back words she so wanted to say.

Courtney came back. "Good night, Mom. It's been a wonderful evening, but I'm going to go soak in the tub. Hope that's okay."

"Of course, and good night, darling." Her fingers held onto her daughter's hand a bit longer than usual, then let her hand slip away. It was so difficult letting a child go and losing a husband.

"I'll have coffee on bright and early."

"You don't need to. I can catch some on my way to work."

"No, I like to do it."

And so it went. Every evening was similar, yet tonight

was different for Courtney.

She turned her stereo on, reveling in the sound of Vince Gill's "If You Ever Have Forever in Mind." Letting the water run high, she hummed as she added three capfuls of lavender bubble bath. Tonight she'd be extravagant.

Later, as Courtney slipped under the thick quilt, she thought first about Steven's penetrating gaze, then his crooked little grin, and smiled.

❧

Work was laborious, as it often was on Mondays. Bob seemed more attentive than usual.

"You're looking good, Courtney." He ran a hand through his dark hair. "Yeah, for a Monday you're looking extremely good."

Courtney looked out the window. "Thank you," she responded. Again she thought of how this was often the only answer one could give.

He came over and touched her shoulder. "How about going to dinner with me after work?"

"Work and pleasure don't mix. Didn't we discuss this before?"

"They can if I say so."

Courtney had always sensed that Bob liked her. When she'd first come to work, he'd invited her to lunch, and she'd refused.

"I just want to get to know you better," he had said then. He'd reached over and touched her face ever so briefly. It had made her uncomfortable.

When he asked her out again and she still refused, he seemed almost angry.

"Mr. Jenkins—"

"Bob," he interrupted, "Bob, please." His dark eyes met

hers, and she looked away. "Is there someone else?"

"Not exactly."

And there hadn't been then. Now there was Steven.

He stalked back into the room and dropped another stack of letters. "I thought you seemed extra attentive today. You can't blame a guy for trying."

"Perhaps you'd like to come to the young adults' group at my church. We have a good time and do worthwhile things," Courtney said. "You could meet some nice women."

He looked at her through dark, narrowed eyes, as if he couldn't believe she'd suggested such a thing. "Listen, I had all the church-going I needed as a kid. No, thank you." He left before she could respond.

"Oh, Lord," Courtney prayed, "help Bob to know that no means no."

He acted rather frosty the rest of the day, and she didn't finish the work until six, an hour later than usual. A bit despondent, she dug Steven's business card out of her purse. What if he was still at work? Somehow she needed to see a smiling face about now.

Courtney applied lipstick and ran a brush through her hair before locking the office.

Sunshine, warm and golden, hit the changing leaves on the rows of trees lining Park Avenue. She liked walking the park blocks in the fall.

Steven had left, but a kid that looked entirely too young to be working there jotted down her name. "He'll see this first thing when he comes in the office." He grabbed a jacket. "Hey, did you say Courtney?"

Courtney smiled. "Yes."

"Hi, I'm Jeff." He held out a hand.

"Trans Am Jeff?" she couldn't help asking.

He nodded. "Yeah, that's me. And I know about you, too." He grinned. "Man, will Steven be mad that he missed you."

Courtney went out the door he held open for her.

"It was just a whim. To come here, I mean."

They rode the elevator down. "I like what Steven's been doing."

"Doing?"

"Yeah. New duds, for one. Says he's looking for another car, too."

Courtney didn't know what to say, so she said nothing.

"Hey, can I give you a lift?"

"That's okay. I took the Max in."

"No problem, but Steven wouldn't like it if I left you stranded. Riding the transit is okay, but don't you get tired of all the stops?"

"Yeah, but it's cheaper than downtown parking."

"Let me take you home. I'll even drive slower than usual." He grinned again.

Finally, Courtney agreed and followed him to a small garage a few blocks away. She did like the Trans Am.

"Steven will be pea green with envy when I tell him I met you and gave you a lift."

Courtney and Jeff had a nice talk, like old friends, as he fought the late-evening traffic. "This is why I don't drive," she said. "I hate the traffic."

Alice was on the porch sipping a tall iced tea when they pulled into the yard. "That wasn't Steven," she said as Courtney turned to wave good-bye.

"No. That's Jeff, Steven's employee. And he insisted on bringing me home. Said Steven would be furious if I was left stranded."

"Well, dear," Alice leaned up for Courtney's kiss on the

cheek, "your life has suddenly become more interesting."

Courtney didn't mention Bob's asking her out. There were things mothers didn't need to know.

"How'd you run into Jeff?" Alice asked, following Courtney into the house.

"I went to Steven's office."

Alice frowned. Never, ever would Alice have gone to a man's office, nor would she have called one on the phone.

The phone rang, as if Courtney's thinking about it caused it to ring.

"Courtney?"

She trembled at the sound of his deep voice. "Yes?"

"Jeff just called me on his cellular and said you'd dropped by the office." There was a long pause. "I hate it that I missed you and can hardly wait for Wednesday. We have good seats."

"I'm so looking forward to it."

By the time she and Steven exchanged pleasantries, Alice had set the table and removed a casserole from the oven.

"I need to go. Call me tomorrow."

As she replaced the receiver, she wondered why her heart was pounding so hard. Everything was moving fast, way too fast.

six

Courtney dressed casual for the baseball game—her first date with Steven, if she didn't count the ice cream after church. She decided on jeans; a pink shirt with pearl buttons, giving it a western look; and a matching denim jacket, one on which her mother had sewn a butterfly patch. After tying her dark hair back with a silver clasp, she looked for her favorite baseball cap.

The cap was from the old Portland Beavers' team that used to play in Civic Stadium. Her father took her to at least half of the games each season, and one year he caught a fly ball. The ball, autographed by the batter, sat in a prominent place on top of her dresser, right next to the cap.

She looked forward to seeing the Portland Rockies play. It might sound like a funny place to go on a date, but she loved sports—any and all sports. Once she'd gone with a guy to a Trail Blazer basketball game and ended up explaining the plays and why fouls were called. Courtney knew this wouldn't be the case with Steven. Last night she'd discovered they had another mutual interest. Monopoly. He'd once stayed up all night playing. That seemed a bit excessive, but one could get caught up in the game. She hadn't played since the nights when Tina used to stay over.

She hummed one of her favorite songs as she put away a stack of clothes from a chair beside the bed. Why had that song come to mind? She sang out loud:

"I love you Lord, and I lift my voice
To worship You, O, my soul, rejoice.
Take joy, my King, in what You hear,
May it be a sweet, sweet sound in Your ear."

Courtney had the run of the upper story since her parents slept on the main floor. Her bedroom faced the front of the house. Her mother's old sewing room was tucked back in a corner at the top of the stairs. The other bedroom was the one Courtney used to dream would belong to her sister. Every year until she was ten, she had asked for a sister for Christmas and for her birthday. Then she had given up and settled on a dog. Ruggles had died just last year, and so far she hadn't replaced him with another. Not that one could ever replace a dog.

An oak bed with a high headboard dominated the center of the spare bedroom. A matching dresser sat under the dormer windows. A photo was on the opposite wall—a ballerina in a pink tutu. Courtney had wanted to dance, to be elegant and dainty, but one needed long legs to be graceful, so her dreams of being a prima ballerina soon faded.

Leaning against the bank of pink-fringed pillows, she spoke aloud. "Mom, you wanted another child so bad. I wonder why you and Daddy didn't adopt again."

Courtney had always known she was adopted, but it hadn't mattered when she was small. She'd been told the story countless times of how her parents had picked her out of all the other babies. She later discovered that wasn't the entire truth, but knew they had told her that to make her feel more special and loved. They'd heard about a young girl who could not keep her baby, and they had offered to adopt her child.

"We paid for her hospitalization and doctor and gave her some money to get back on her feet," her mother had explained.

"What did she look like?" Courtney had asked.

Alice had looked surprised at the question. "Honey, we never met her. A lawyer took care of the proceedings."

"But didn't you care? Didn't you want to know what I would look like?"

Her mother had taken her hands, pulling her to her bosom. "We just wanted a baby. We would have taken you if you'd been sickly, handicapped, or multiracial. We'd tried for five years and the doctor said I'd never conceive."

Courtney had pressed on, but her mother really didn't know anything about the family or their background. Maybe it wouldn't have mattered, but a girl at school knew her birth mother and they got together twice a year. Her friend had curly hair, just like her birth mother. What Courtney wouldn't give to know just that much.

"You are so precious to us," Alice had said. "You've seen the birth certificate and the little gown you were wearing after you were born."

And Courtney had. They were tucked into the large trunk in the sewing room. She went often to look at the birth certificate, reading it as if it would suddenly give her a clue to her real identity. The homemade gown had a pink crocheted edging at the bottom and at the wrists. It was packed in clear plastic to preserve it. She often thought of the mother who had made this nightgown for her baby.

"If you really must continue searching, you may need to go back to southern Illinois where you were born," her mother had finally suggested. "Maybe you can find out something there. Your father was stationed at Scott Air

Force Base and got out of the service there so we could return to Oregon."

Courtney had held her mother close. "Mom, I do need to go there. Please understand. I love you very much but need to find this out."

Alice had pulled the hair back from Courtney's face. "Of course. I always knew the day would come when you'd want to know."

She thought about her father. She missed him so terribly and wondered why it had never been as imperative to find her real father as it was to find her birth mother. She recalled that half year of illness. Weakness had overtaken her body, and she had been tutored at home. Tests, hundreds of them, it seemed, had been taken. Nothing. Lots of things were ruled out. Diabetes. Multiple sclerosis. Anemia. Mono. Epilepsy. She had none of the symptoms for epilepsy, but the doctor was thorough. Then, miraculously, with everyone at church praying for her, she started back up the road to recovery. Soon she was her old self, her energy restored. She returned to school that fall and even played basketball when the season started.

"It's amazing," Dr. Bell had said with a shake of his snow-white head. "I can't explain it, but there are a lot of things I cannot explain. Guess I have to say it's an answer to prayer." He patted Courtney's shoulder.

"She's well again and that's the main thing," Alice Adams said. "Our prayers were answered."

At first Courtney had been hesitant, fearful that the illness would return, but it did not. And soon she relaxed and let life happen again. Yet in the back of her mind, questions remained. What if she did get sick again? What if she was a carrier of whatever this disease was and it could hit her unborn child, should she marry in the future? No. She could not, would not, let the matter rest. She must find out about her medical background—must find her birth mother to get the answers.

It had been anything but easy. Every door slammed in her face. The Internet, which most said was helpful, did not help with her search. That was when she knew the only thing left to do, the only stone unturned, was to return to the place of her birth.

❧

Courtney heard a car in the driveway and looked out the window to see an old black car pull up. She laughed. Steven was right. It was in despicable condition, yet she had to admire someone who would even drive such a car, let alone pick up a date in it. No wonder he had borrowed his friend's Trans Am last week for the trip to the ice cream store.

The doorbell rang just as Courtney descended the stairs. She opened it before her mother did, though her mother always said a woman needed to keep a man waiting for at least five minutes.

"That's lame, Mom!" Courtney had retorted. "I don't think it appears too eager; it shows you are considerate."

So much for that discussion.

Steven smiled and started to step forward. Courtney wondered if he was going to put his arms around her or what. He stepped back and removed his baseball cap, holding it in his hand, seemingly more nervous than Sunday night after church.

"You look like you're ready for a baseball game," he finally said.

"I am." She removed her cap and hit his. "The Beavers here."

"San Diego Padres here."

"We don't match."

"I know, but who cares?"

Alice appeared and held out her hand. "Nice to see you again, Steven. And I do hope the Rockies win."

"You could come along, if you wanted," Steven said.

She laughed. "Me? No. I'm not the sports enthusiast my daughter is or the one my husband was. You two go and have a good time."

Courtney thought about Steven's willingness to include her mother in their plans. It showed a thoughtfulness she hadn't found in most men. He had been taught well by someone. She knew little about his growing-up years or he about hers. That would give them things to talk about for at least two more dates.

The stadium was nearly full. The Portland Rockies had loyal fans, though they were just an A-team. Courtney discovered that Steven liked the center bleachers best for a good, all-around view. If the game got tight, they'd move over closer to home plate.

"Popcorn before we sit?" Steven asked.

"Later," Courtney said. "I had a late dinner."

"Me, too."

He led the way, turning back to capture her hand, and they found the perfect spot and sat—but not for long. Courtney was out of her seat more than she was in it.

"Do you always get this excited at ball games?" Steven grinned. He was clearly amused by her enthusiasm.

Her face flushed suddenly. "I hope I'm not embarrassing you."

"Hardly." He studied her profile, thinking how much he enjoyed seeing someone having fun. Courtney was the type one could get to know easily, one you could enjoy being with. He never wanted the night to end. "I happen to like girls who are athletic."

"And I like *men,*" she said, "who like sports."

At the seventh-inning stretch, with the score tied at 4, they decided to get popcorn and peanuts and two colas.

"Let's drive around after the game," Steven said.

"It'll be dark," Courtney said. "Does that matter?"

"No. How about going where we can see the city lights?"

"I know the very place," Courtney said. "There's a fantastic view. You won't believe it until you see it."

"Okay. Sounds great."

The Rockies won in the ninth, a stolen base on an error by Spokane. As they trickled out of the stadium, Steven stopped to buy two hats. "So we can match," he said, putting one on Courtney's head.

"Hey, thanks! I needed a new one. It's a long way to my spot, but on my end of town."

"Lead me on."

They drove across town and started driving up a large hill.

When they came to the closed gate, Courtney let out a disappointed, "Oh, no. I should have known. Of course they close the gates at dusk."

"A cemetery?" Steven sounded incredulous.

"It's Willamette National Cemetery, and my father is buried here. You can see out west over the entire city and the view is fantastic. He has a very special spot."

Steven stopped the car. "You miss him very much, don't you?"

Courtney nodded, not daring to meet Steven's gaze. "He was a special man, a special father. We had no idea his heart was bad. The doctor said he undoubtedly had had symptoms, but he'd ignored them."

"Men hate doctors."

"So do some women." She grinned as he reached over and took her hand.

"I think I could spend the night here, just listening to you talk about your family and your life. You definitely have an effect on me, Courtney." He pulled her a bit closer. She felt herself leaning, afraid to let her guard down, as he was affecting her, also. No longer a teenager who had to worry about a dark night on a hill with a romantic moon beaming down, she suddenly felt vulnerable.

"I don't know a thing about you." She pulled back, though she hadn't wanted to. "What were your growing-up years like?"

"Grams ran it all. The ranch. The house. Me. But nobody ever minded. She was loving and special, sort of like your father was. You could depend on her. You knew she had your best interests at heart."

"How long ago did you lose her?"

"I was off to college, my freshman year, when the call came from a neighbor. It was the longest, most painful two-hour drive I ever had to make."

"From?"

"The University of Oregon."

"It's a nice campus. My father graduated from there. We went to sing once with another youth group."

"I played guitar in a band on weekends."

"You play guitar?" Courtney was immediately interested. "I had no idea you played. We've been looking for someone for our meetings. Just a few songs before the actual meeting starts."

"It's been a long time." His arm went around her, and he pulled her close again. "I think I could pick it up again pretty quick."

"Oh, Steven, I'm sure you could."

He started to lean toward her, but she pulled away. "Let's not start something we don't want to stop."

"You're right." He thumped the steering wheel. "I agree." An awkward silence followed.

"I'm looking forward to working in the soup kitchen," he said finally. "Not sure if I'll be of any help, but I'll give it a try."

"There's nothing to it. Scoop up the food. Smile at the customers. Tell them God loves them."

"You preach to them?"

"Not really preach. Some don't say anything, but I like to tell them how I feel about them and how I know God feels."

"You're pretty amazing, Courtney."

"No, I'm not." She met his gaze. "I think I'd better have you take me home." Her voice trembled, and she felt all quivery inside. She thought she'd been in love with a boy once, but never, ever had she felt like this. And from the way Steven looked at her, she knew he was feeling the same thing.

"I don't want to wait until Saturday. Do you suppose you could meet me on Friday for dinner? You're not far from the main downtown area. How about Brewster's?"

"Yeah. I'd like that."

He drove down the curvy, windy road toward town and back on to 92nd.

"I'll even buy."

"It's a date," she said, turning on the car radio to see

what kind of music was playing. She found a George Strait ballad and started singing along.

"I like to hear you sing."

She looked over and smiled. Too soon, they were at Courtney's home. They said a quick good night and she disappeared into the house.

Driving home, Steven whispered a prayer. "Thank You, Lord, for giving me a little push in the right direction—and thank You for Grams, too."

seven

Brewster's was the best place in town for ribs. They also had a great salad bar and terrific atmosphere. Steven needed to unwind. It had been a horrendous day.

Courtney left the office ten minutes late because Bob asked her to answer an E-mail that had come through at five.

She sighed. It seemed that no matter how hard she tried, she was always late for appointments and dinner engagements and barely on time for church service.

By the time she'd walked the four blocks to the restaurant, her hair was windblown. She entered the rest room, applied a touch of pale pink lipstick, and brushed her hair out. She pulled it back and put clips on each side.

Brewster's buzzed with activity as usual. It was a crazy, interesting place. Each table had a small tub of peanuts. People cracked the peanuts, throwing the shells on the floor. The décor was the '50s, which was the rage in Portland right now. Her mother loved going to anything that catered to her age group. She'd have to bring her here sometime. Of course, the peanut shells underfoot might bother her.

Steven had a table in the back and waved her over. He stood when she walked up. "I thought you might have forgotten," he said, looking intently at her.

Forget? How could I possibly forget? She thought the words, but stopped herself from blurting them out.

He helped her with her chair while she ran a hand through her hair. It was a nervous habit she had tried to break in the past. "Sorry I'm late. It's all Bob's fault."

Steven grinned. "I hope you asked for a raise."

"Not hardly. He's struggling, you know."

"As we all are."

She took the menu and ordered a cola from the waitress. Steven was all business at times, and she wanted to just forget work. She would much rather he talk about himself or about his hobbies. "Bob is in no position to give me a raise," she said.

Steven suddenly reached for her hand. "Sorry. That's none of my business."

She smiled reassuringly at him as the waitress set down her cola. "I'll have my usual," she told the waitress. "Unlimited salad bar." Salad bars were her thing. It seemed she could never get enough greens. Her mother used to kid her, saying she was half rabbit. As a teenager she could visualize that; but which half was the rabbit?

Steven grinned. "If I never looked at another salad, I'd be only too happy. I need something more substantial. I'll try the soup of the day, then an order of ribs."

He cracked open a peanut and handed it to her. "Aren't you going after your salad?"

She took the peanut. "In due time. I'll wait until closer to the time when your ribs will be done."

He leaned forward and grinned again. "You think of everything, don't you?"

Her gaze locked on his. "Perhaps. Is that a bad trait?"

"Hardly."

"Steven," she started, then paused, not sure when this discussion needed to take place. She decided now seemed like a good time. "Do you know that I'm adopted?"

He glanced up, his face revealing nothing. "No, I didn't."

Courtney leaned forward. "It affects the way I think and plan and I just thought you might like to know."

"Have you always known?"

She nodded. "From the first."

"And you felt?"

"Happy to be chosen. To be loved and cared for by two wonderful people."

"And now?" Steven wasn't sure why, but for some reason he knew her answer was going to involve him.

"It's just that I need to find out about my background. I've been searching for the past four years."

The soup came, steaming with a pleasant fragrance. He picked up the spoon, never taking his eyes from Courtney's face.

She touched his arm. "I hope you don't mind if I ask a blessing first."

His face turned red. "No, of course not. Sorry I didn't think of it."

After she had offered the blessing and he had burned his mouth on the first spoonful, he asked why there had been no results after all that time.

"I don't know. It's been ultra frustrating."

"I assume you don't mind talking about this—"

"Quite the contrary. I *want* to discuss it. It helps." She met his level gaze while toying with the straw. "In fact, I'm planning on a trip to the town in Illinois where I was born. I'm leaving in two weeks."

"Leaving?" he choked, then sat there with a dismayed look on his face.

"You're not saying anything."

"I guess I don't know what to say. I'm not wanting you to go, if that's what you're wondering about."

She looked away, realizing she didn't want to be away from Steven, either, and for a second doubting she really needed to go. But it was because of how she was feeling about Steven that the quest had become even more crucial. How could she even think of a permanent relationship when she didn't know what she was bringing into it?

"I never knew my mother and barely remember my dad," Steven said then.

"But what happened?" She'd always heard that everyone had problems; you just thought you were the only one.

"I think I mentioned at the ball game about Mom dying and Dad, unable to stand the loss, took off. Thank God I had Grams and the cattle ranch in Redmond."

"But how'd you get into computers?"

He pushed the empty soup bowl aside. "Because I didn't take to farming and cows and riding the range, to Grams's dismay."

"Oh, really? I can see you now, roping one of those little dogies."

"And how do you know about *dogies* if you've never lived on a ranch?"

"I read books, you know." She was teasing him now. Steven was too serious. Courtney had grown up with a father who teased constantly. It was good in a way. Perhaps. She tended not to take things seriously and had gotten in trouble on her first job when she told a customer the hamburgers were made from the best ground buffalo.

Courtney got up and walked toward the salad bar. "Just wanted to see how gullible you are," she called over her shoulder.

"Men are supposed to do the teasing," he said when she returned with a plate heaping with salad greens, tomatoes, cucumbers, green peas, cheese sticks, sliced boiled egg, and blue cheese dressing in a mound on top.

"True," she said. "That's how it works most of the time."

They talked about the week coming up and when he could see her again.

"Choir practice is Thursday at seven. Why don't you join the choir?"

"If you heard me sing, you wouldn't ask that question."

She stabbed a crouton. "You're going to play guitar, and that's more important than the choir any day."

The ribs came, stacked high on a platter. He grabbed his fork.

"Want to take in another Rockies game?" Steven asked when he'd finished the last rib.

"I'd love to."

She felt comfortable with him. He was also the first date she'd ever told about her background. She felt herself liking him more and more but wasn't sure about his commitment to God. She could not fathom being linked to someone who did not share the faith with her.

The evening ended too soon, and she lingered a bit longer than usual in his car.

"I'll see you tomorrow morning?"

"I'll be there." He leaned over and kissed her cheek. "Thanks for a fun time."

Later that evening, long after the house was straightened and she had decided what to wear the next day, she thought of Steven. She loved how his eyes crinkled up on the edges when he smiled at her. She also liked the way he was a gentleman and didn't assume she wanted his arm around her.

He hadn't tried to kiss her yet, and that meant even more. Most men wanted more, so much more, on a date. She liked his old-fashioned manners.

Courtney came back downstairs to spend some time with Alice. She had volunteered at the local hospital that day and often wanted to talk about her day.

"I met a woman today who found her mother after a lengthy search." Alice leaned over and touched Courtney's arm. "She says you need to do it."

"Do it?"

"Go to Illinois."

Courtney leaned over and hugged her mother. "Thanks for telling me this. It's almost like a sign."

Her mother nodded. "That's what I thought, dear. A sign that God is with us and will help you and keep you safe."

Long after the house was quiet and Courtney lay looking out the window at the stars in the sky, she thought again of Steven and what this could mean should she find her birth mother. "Thank You, God," she prayed, "for caring so much about us. About me."

And then, with another thought about Steven linking his arm in hers, she finally closed her eyes.

eight

Courtney had wondered more than once if someday she might not come across a relative. The fact that her adoptive parents had left Illinois, coming west to Oregon, made the possibility "extremely unlikely," as Tina put it.

"You worry about things that probably won't happen, and I never worry about things when I probably should," Tina said.

The two had met early Saturday morning, grabbing a quick cup of coffee and a cinnamon roll at a café a few blocks from the soup kitchen.

"I'm not worried, just thinking about it," Courtney retorted. "By the way, how are you doing?" Her hand touched the firm round shape of Tina's stomach. Somehow she couldn't even imagine how it must feel, having someone grow inside you.

"Good," Tina said, slathering more butter on her roll. "The weight is good, but if I have very many more mornings like this, the pounds will pour on."

"It's so good to see you," Courtney said. "We never get together, except at church."

"I know."

Courtney leaned forward. "You remember the new guy at church on Sunday?"

"The one you kept looking at all through service?"

Courtney blushed. "Yes."

"You're seeing him, aren't you!" Tina's face lit up. "I

could tell he was coming on to you."

"He signed up to help at the soup kitchen. We've had dinner at Brewster's, went to a Rockies game, and also drove up by the cemetery, and had ice cream, and—"

"Whoa, girl!" Tina rolled her eyes. "Is this fast or what?"

"Oh, I know, but something tells me he might be the right one."

"What does Alice think?"

"She likes him. He's always asking her to come with us."

"And your search?" Tina had polished off her roll and dabbed at her face with her napkin. "What's happening about that?"

Courtney looked serious. "I'm leaving for Illinois sometime soon."

"Leaving? You can't leave now."

"Yes, I can. It's the only way I'll ever find myself and know about my background."

"And what if Mr. Right doesn't want to wait?"

Courtney leaned back, pushing the roll aside. She wasn't hungry now. "That's a problem, all right."

"I'd think twice. Like I've said before, it doesn't take having a baby to be a mother." Tina pushed her chair back, placing the side of her hand over her midsection. "Everything sits right here." She grinned. "Just you wait, missy. One day you'll be able to experience this, too."

"I want to experience that, you know. And as far as Alice, I've always considered her my real mother. She loves me. Yet somewhere," her voice broke, "somewhere a woman gave me up to be adopted. Did she want to do that, or was she coerced into giving me up? Was she happy to be rid of me, or does she lie awake at night, stare at the moon, and wonder where in this vast universe her little girl is?"

"Do you still carry that picture in your wallet?"

"You mean the one with Mom and me in matching red, white, and blue bonnets?"

"Yeah, that one."

Courtney dug it out and handed it over. "It always reminds me of how much I've been loved and how much I have to be thankful for. Sometimes I ask God to forgive me for wanting to find my birth mother. Something just pushes me on."

Tina looked at the photo. "I love the smug smile on Alice's face." She looked at her watch. "We better get a move on."

Courtney grabbed the bill and the two friends made their way to Northwest Third Street, making plans for a shopping trip after the kitchen was closed.

Tina took her volunteer duties seriously. She started setting out the bread and cookies. "Yum, potato soup," she said, taking a spoon and tasting it. "Has lots of bacon and onion in it, too."

"You can't go wrong on potato," Courtney said. She set the bread on a plate with tongs beside it. Someone always served the food. If they didn't, some took more than their share and others did without.

"Someone brought several of those boxes from Costco," Tina said. "Look. The cookies are frosted."

"They look good," Courtney said, grabbing one, though she wasn't hungry.

"I thought the new guy—what's-his-name—was coming."

"It's Steven," Courtney said. "Steven with a *V*."

"Well, I wonder where he is, Steven with a V," Tina said. "Looks like he isn't going to make it."

Courtney's heart sank. Something must have come up.

"It's time," Tina called. "C'mon, Courtney, stand by the bread."

The door opened and the people started pushing through. Most had on well-worn clothes that smelled from not enough washing. With hair hanging in strings, some in dreadlocks, they shuffled to the table. Most wore smiles and mumbled thank-yous.

Courtney had finally gotten used to this part, but it was difficult. The first inclination was to invite people home to have an honest-to-goodness bath, to look in the closet for an old sweatshirt and pants to give someone, or to offer a decent bed for the night.

"You can't do that," Tina said. "How would you know which one to choose? How do you know you can trust them?"

" 'Inasmuch as ye have done it unto me,' " Courtney had started reciting the familiar passage.

"I know. We are doing what we can and, for the most part, the people have their little community right here and would not fit in with so-called regular life."

The line finally dwindled down and then Gerta came in. Gerta, a perceptive and talkative old woman, had once been a psychologist. "I know people," she always said. "Can tell an honest person when I see one." She also liked to think she could make predictions.

Gerta flashed her toothless, happy grin. "So? Did my prediction come true from last month?"

Courtney looked puzzled as she tried to remember what Gerta had said.

"I don't remember."

"You were going to meet a man," Tina said. "I remember that much."

"I meet lots of men," Courtney said.

Gerta laughed. "Ah, but I did not say that. And from the

look in your eyes, I see you are thinking of a certain someone."

Courtney busied herself refilling the butter dish, preferring not to respond.

"Trust me; I will come in one day and you will not be here. You will be off with your young man on a honeymoon."

"Oh, Gerta, dream on," Courtney said, hoping someone else would come in. And when she looked up, someone did. Steven. Her heart caught in her throat. Tina looked up and saw him at the same time.

"You're late," Tina said. "We're just about ready to wrap it up."

"I brought carrots. All peeled." He set a huge bowl of carrots on the table. "Surely someone will want them." His gaze found Courtney's.

"What happened?" Courtney finally asked.

"Got hung up with a problem. It was a rush call from a large business firm. I thought I'd finish in plenty of time."

Gerta, who had started off with her tray, stopped and looked back. "See? Didn't my prediction come true?"

Courtney knew it was coincidence. No way could Gerta know how she felt about Steven.

"I'll help clean up. That's permissible, isn't it?" Steven asked.

"Another crew is coming on for the cleanup," Tina said.

"Then I'll stay and it'll all get done that much faster."

Courtney felt him looking at her as she busied herself with the empty bread plate.

"I want you to go gallery shopping with me. Do you have the afternoon free?"

"I—have plans," Courtney started, but Tina was there, pushing her gently.

"We can go another time. I really should get home to finish cleaning out the room for the baby's crib."

Courtney couldn't remember putting anything away or wiping the table off or waving good-bye to Gerta as she shuffled off. Steven had come. And she laughed as she saw him with rolled-up sleeves, proceeding to wash the soup pot. Her heart told her again that he was the right one. There was no doubt about it now. She knew, just as she knew she was God's child and He had her interests at heart.

"I'll be ready to go shopping whenever you are," she called from the doorway.

nine

Courtney helped Steven select a Monet print, a water scene in greens, blues, and purples entitled "Cape Martin," for one wall in the living room. For the opposite wall, they chose an Eric Wiegardt watercolor called "Sign of Spring," featuring the side of an old building with ironwork and a hanging basket filled with blue and red flowers; it was a nice contrast to the Monet in color and style. Wiegardt was a Washington State artist and that was close enough to be local. A humorous Norman Rockwell for the bathroom concluded the purchases, though Steven wanted a glass creation for his coffee table.

"Think I've extended my budget for the month," he said, taking Courtney's hand. "And thank you for helping me choose."

"What else do you need to do?" Courtney asked as he put the wrapped paintings in his car.

"I think it's time for fun now. There's a bluegrass concert playing tonight down at Waterfront Park. Let's take a picnic lunch and a blanket and go. That is, if you like bluegrass."

"If it's a picnic and an outdoor concert, it wouldn't matter what was playing," Courtney replied.

After picking up fried chicken, potato salad, and two large sugar cookies at a corner deli, they joined the large crowd at the park along the Willamette River.

"The last vestiges of summer," Courtney said, hugging her knees up under her. The sky was a powder blue and the early evening breeze came in from the river, cooling them off.

Steven nibbled on his cookie. "I like being with you." He reached over and took her hand.

"Thank you," Courtney murmured. "And the same to you."

"I want to see you tomorrow and the next day and the next."

Courtney met his steady gaze and wanted to say the same thing, but there were too many unknowns in her life just now. How could she commit to Steven?

❧

They continued to date as summer blended into fall, and Courtney kept putting off her trip. Each week Steven played his guitar, and one night he opened up the Sunday evening service with "Amazing Grace." Courtney's voice lifted high and strong with the rest of the congregation, the volume increasing as they sang the last verse:

"When we've been there ten thousand years,
  Bright shining as the sun,
We've no less days to sing God's praise,
  Than when we first begun."

That night Steven made a public declaration of his faith. He did not like making speeches but had a few things he wanted to share with his friends at the community church.

"I have led a happy life and been blessed many ways by God. He gave me Grams—God rest her soul—when I lost my parents at a young age. She was instrumental in teaching me right from wrong, reading me God's Word, and seeing that I attended Sunday school. Yet my faith until now has all been lip service." Steven glanced around at the faces of the people listening to and watching him. "I didn't realize that one does not go to heaven by works, but by faith. And I have faith and believe that God sent His Son to save me, to make me whole. And I just thank this congregation for taking me in and loving me and caring about me. My favorite Scripture is from Proverbs 3:5: 'Trust in the Lord with all your heart and lean not on your own understanding.' "

He sat down amid cheers and claps. His face wasn't even red, and he felt much better after his testimony. Courtney reached over and took his hand. Her gesture made him realize how much he loved her, how much he wanted to make her his wife.

"Let's go celebrate afterwards," he whispered in her ear. He had something for her and could hardly bear to wait.

She nodded and squeezed his hand again.

Courtney thought she'd prepared herself for what seemed inevitable. She wondered if women usually sensed when a man was about to propose. For her, it was as if God told her the first time she'd seen Steven sitting in the second pew that this man was going to become very important in her life.

They raced to the Ford, hand in hand, with Courtney giggling. She studied his profile, liking the good strong jawline, the way his nose angled perfectly, the short hair, his ears not too large, yet not small. She had his facial features memorized. She loved Steven. It had always been there, perhaps, but a sudden feeling of love so overwhelmed her she could hardly breathe.

"Where to?" he asked. "You're my guide, you know."

She kept looking at him and didn't answer.

"What are you looking at?" His hand reached over.

"You." Her fingers reached up and touched his chin. "But, we'd better get out of the parking lot before everyone talks about us."

"I repeat, where to? We need to talk. Do you know a place that's on the quiet side?"

Courtney nodded. "Donovan's. It's not far. We could sit in one of the back booths. Then later I want to go up to Rocky Butte and look out over Portland. It's the best place for stargazing. The first time Mom went out with Dad, it was on the back of his Harley and they went up to Rocky Butte."

"*Your mom?* Alice rode on a motorcycle?"

Courtney laughed. "Yeah, my mom. I somehow can't imagine it, either, but I guess she was adventuresome then."

"I've never owned a motorcycle," Steven said. "Never wanted one. I was more into tractors than trucks."

"Then old, rundown, beat-up cars," Courtney added.

"Now, don't make fun of my car. It might just hear you and stop running."

The little café on Skidmore was busy, but Courtney said it was always busy. She promised they made the best hamburgers, so that's what they ordered.

"I brought something along," Steven said, putting his cola down. "It's been on my mind and heart for several days, and I can't wait a second longer." He reached inside his pants pocket and brought out a small, velvet-covered box. Courtney held her breath.

"Go on. Open it."

Courtney hadn't expected anything like this. "Steven! A ring! I had no idea." It was a beautiful, oval pink stone in a platinum setting. "It's beautiful! What kind of stone is this?"

"Alexandrite. It belonged to my grandmother."

"Oh, Steven." Her breath came out in one long swoosh. "I couldn't possibly accept this. It's a family heirloom, and I'm far too careless with things. You just don't know."

"No." His tone was firm. "I want you to have it. I want you to be my lifetime partner, Courtney. I love you. Surely you know that by now." He took the ring from the box and gently placed it on her finger. "For always. You and me. You, me, and God."

She looked at him through sudden tears. "I love it, Steven, and I love you, too, but I'm not sure that I can say yes."

"Because of the trip to Illinois to find your birth mother."

"Yes, I'm leaving soon. I told Bob already."

"I want to go with you."

"No, I must do this on my own." She started to take the ring off, but he stopped her, taking her hand in his.

"No," he insisted, "it's yours. I want you to have it, no matter what. For always. I want you to wear the ring. I also want to help."

"I appreciate that more than I can say."

"Grams gave me this on her deathbed," he told her, his finger going over the stone. "She said when I found the right woman that I'd know, and I was to give it to her to wear with as much pride and honor as Grams had always had."

"And I will wear it with pride," Courtney said.

Later they drove up to Rocky Butte and looked out over the star-studded sky.

So far their dates had been with others, except the ball game that first night. Movies, playing tennis, the drive out to Multnomah Falls—all with Tina and Mike or the group as a whole. They'd been careful not to be alone as Courtney admitted right off that she didn't believe in relations before marriage. And it could be tempting. She thought of the paper of abstention she'd signed back in junior high after attending several Wednesday night meetings, all about staying chaste until marriage.

They sat on the stone fence, Steven's arm slipping around her shoulder. "This is my kind of night. My kind of girl."

"Oh, Steven. I wish I knew who I was. I wish I'd had success before now. You must understand why I have to go to Illinois. Not even my love for you can stop me. In fact, that's the reason I'm more determined to find out. I must find myself. What am I bringing into this relationship?"

"You're bringing love, caring, and a beautiful attitude. What more could a fellow want?"

Their eyes met and held. Then she pulled away ever so slightly.

"To know something about his wife, the mother of his children, to know about her background."

"Obviously it's more important to you than to me."

"How can I totally commit?"

"Totally commit?" His gaze burned into hers, never leaving her face.

"I mean like marriage."

"Of course marriage is uppermost in my mind."

"Oh, Steven, I know. It's just that I *must* know this first before settling on a date or making plans. . . ." Her voice trailed off.

"But you will keep the ring?"

"Yes, Steven." She held it up, letting the artificial light catch the sparkle from the gem. "It's almost too beautiful to wear, though."

"You think it's better stuck in a safety deposit box where nobody can see it?"

"I'm leaving for Illinois end of this month," she said. "I gave notice to Bob on Friday."

"I see."

"You know how I felt about it. This isn't a surprise."

"Please let me come with you."

"Steven, you can't. You have a business to run."

"So?"

"This is something I must do on my own. I don't even want Mom to come."

"How about Tina?"

"Mike would have a stroke. Besides, there's the baby." Courtney pushed her half-eaten pie away. "Here, finish this if you want."

He didn't want it. "I don't like you going off alone to someplace you've never been before."

"I'll take my cellular, call you every day, sleep only in safe, well-lighted places. Not talk to strangers—"

"Stop!" He held his hand up. "I think you have it covered."

They left and Alice arrived home as they did. Courtney rushed over and held her hand in front of her mother's face. "It's a ring, Mom. An engagement ring."

"Oh, darling, that's wonderful." She hugged Courtney, her eyes meeting Steven's over the top of Courtney's head. She stood a good six inches taller. "I am so happy for both of you. Come on in, Steven. This calls for a toast!"

"I really must go, Alice. Busy day, big contract tomorrow." He came over and hugged his mother-in-law to be. "It's been a busy night."

Courtney watched as Steven's car backed up and until his taillights disappeared around the corner. She watched with a happy, yet heavy, heart. She had hurt him; she knew she had, but she had to be aboveboard with everything. It was just the way she'd always been.

"Courtney, dear, aren't you coming in?"

Courtney stared into the sky, thrilling to the cascade of stars that covered every square inch of it. Her life had suddenly taken on a new dimension. Soon, very soon, she prayed, she'd be an old married woman like Tina. But first things first.

The time had come. Tomorrow she'd make the plane reservations.

ten

Once Courtney made up her mind about something, there was no changing it. She *would* go to Illinois. She *would* begin the search on foot. Alice was adamant that she, too, should go.

"I'll worry about you every second you're gone."

"Mom, you've always worried about me and here I am, age twenty-three, healthy and strong—"

"And strong-willed, I might add."

"You wouldn't want me any other way."

Alice sighed. "No, I guess it wouldn't be you. I swear you're more like your father every day." They both laughed.

"You always used to say that when I was little. It's probably the first thing I have written in my diary."

"And it was true."

"But who knows who I take after?"

Alice stood, putting her shoulders back. "You know what they say about children. The first five years are the most formative. It doesn't matter who gave birth to you; who raised you gave you the principles you now live by."

"Oh, I know that, Mom. Truly I do." Courtney leaned over and hugged her mother hard. "I have never forgotten that, as well as the nights you were at my bedside when I was sick. No mother could have given more. No mother could be loved more."

They clung to each other, tears mingling.

"I don't want to see you hurt."

"God is with me."

"And Steven? Why not take him up on his offer? He says Jeff can run the business for a few days."

"And what if it takes the whole two weeks? It could, you know."

She held up the ring. It was still unbelievable that she was wearing it. It sparkled on her finger. She'd never met Grams, but she knew what a wonderful woman she had to have been. Not only was Steven goal-oriented, precise, methodical—all things Courtney was not—he was tender, gentle, and considerate. And that one fact made him more dear to her than she could have ever thought possible.

"Women, the gentler sex," he had said, almost jokingly, just the night before as they had sipped malts at their favorite ice cream store, the place where their relationship had started. Of course, church was where it really began.

"I don't think of myself that way, but I do know that God intends for the man to be head of the household and if that makes woman the gentler sex, so be it."

"I still want to tag along, for moral support, if nothing else."

"I have to do this, Steven, and until I get some answers, I cannot set a date for our wedding."

He reached out, touching the side of her face. "I am trying to understand, really I am, but it's difficult. I cannot imagine you being so far away, where I can't get to you in ten minutes as I can now. What if you don't find out anything? Or," he added, his brow furrowed, "what if you find out something you don't want to know?"

"I'll handle it when and if that occasion arises. God is with me; don't forget. He's brought me through many things in my life; He won't desert me now."

They had discussed Courtney's illness on the second date. Steven had understood since he did not know his own mother, but at least he knew who she was and therein was the difference.

"I'll miss you."

"And me, you."

"And you'll call every night?"

She smiled, taking his hand again. "Absolutely every night. At eight P.M., as you requested. Keep in mind it will be ten there."

"What if you run out of time and you reach a dead end?"

Courtney nodded. "I've thought of that possibility many, many times and will cross that bridge if and when I get to it. I like to think positive about this."

He held her hand up, gazing at the ring. "It sure looks better on your finger than it did sitting in that box."

"I love it, but I've told you that a dozen times."

"At least."

She closed her eyes, wondering if this was really happening. She thought of Bob's parting shot yesterday.

"Come away with me, Court. We'll go to the West Indies or Fiji or wherever you want. Just the two of us. I'll take you away from this. I'll love and cherish you forever."

She'd almost burst out laughing. How could he even say such things to her when they'd never dated, never talked about important things as she and Steven had? Bob was in love with the idea of being in love. His so-called passion was big and important to him, but he didn't know God and didn't comprehend why God was front and foremost in her life.

"You won't find your birth mother," he'd said.

"I don't want to hear it."

She had set a sheaf of papers on his desk. "I'm sure the temp will work out well."

Courtney thought, as she gathered things from her desk, that she might not come back. Oh, she wouldn't leave him in the lurch, but she doubted that she could ever really work for him again. She now wished she had taken extra schooling so she could be a full-fledged legal assistant, have her own office, and not have to take orders from someone like Bob.

The parting had been anything but amiable. Bob had grabbed at her, as if making a last-ditch effort to keep her from going.

"I love you, Courtney. I have since the day you walked in that door."

"Yeah, sure."

"You don't believe me."

"You're right; I don't."

"If you had given me half a chance I would have proven it."

"I'll be in touch, Bob."

❧

Now she was surveying her room, wondering if she'd packed enough clothes. Would they be suitable? Would she be too warm? Or would it be cold there now that fall had come?

She pulled the flowered curtain back and stared out the window.

So many times she had done this over the years. Somehow she wondered if things would ever be the same again. She could see her mother selling the home and moving in with Agnes. Courtney wondered if she could bear this home going to a complete stranger who didn't know all the secrets, all the laughter, and all the tears that had been shed here. To her, a house was a home, a holder of emotions and memories. Many wonderful memories had been made here.

She heard his car before she saw it. The old Ford. Steven said he was still shopping for the "best buy." But she admired that in him. It was one of his good qualities.

"I might have a better car when you get back," he'd said last night. His breath was warm on her neck, and she knew he was about to kiss her. They'd been careful not to be alone for long because desire mounted inside them, threatening to take over.

"I kind of like this car," Courtney had said.

He'd looked incredulous. "You do?"

"Sure." She grinned. "I have to go in through your side and it's rather difficult to crawl clear over, so as long as I get the seat belt fastened, I'm okay, and I'm closer than if I got in on my side."

He'd laughed then. "You make me so happy, Courtney; I can't believe it. God is so good. I've been praying for the success of this trip."

She'd touched his lips with her cool fingers. "I know you have, and I thank you for it."

They had parted, but now he was here, taking her to the airport. Once she arrived at Lambert Airport in St. Louis, a good fifty miles from the area she'd go to in Illinois, she'd pick up the rental car, then be on her way. She could hardly wait.

Alice had been crying, though she tried to put up a brave front.

Courtney took her mother into her arms. "Mom, I am coming back. You know that, don't you?"

"What if your real mother wants you to stay?"

"I won't stay. What do I know about Illinois? Besides, I have two people right here I love more than life itself. And second, *you* are my real mother." She leaned over and kissed Alice's cheek.

"I just wish you weren't going alone."

"Are you worried about protecting me or worried that I really would choose to stay?" Somehow Courtney couldn't quite believe that would be something her mother would worry about, but Alice was known for her fidgeting and worrying ways. Her husband had chided her about it more than once. His last words to her had been, "Don't worry."

"Every time someone tells me not to worry, something terrible happens," Alice said now. "Remember your father—"

"I know. I was thinking that very thing."

Steven came back for the last small bag and took Courtney's hand. "Come. We'd better get to the airport."

She smiled. They had more than an hour, but Steven felt better if he arrived early. Someday that flat tire might just happen, too.

"I feel like your mother," he said once they were in the car, after the last, frantic wave at Alice. "How can I live without you for two weeks?"

"I may be back in a week, you never know."

"At least I'll hear your voice."

Courtney half-heartedly watched as Steven drove through the midafternoon traffic. He had insisted on parking and seeing her on the plane and would wait until it took off, then would go back to the office. She would feel safe just knowing he was praying for her, along with church members and, of course, her mother. She did hope—oh, how she hoped—this trip would bring the desired results.

eleven

Steven watched until the airplane was a mere speck in the deep blue sky. He felt a tremendous loss, one greater almost than when he'd left the hospital after Grams died. What if Courtney didn't come back? What if the plane crashed? What if she had a change of heart after finding her birth mother? These discoveries could be tragic. While Courtney thought she would have the answers and could now go on with wedding plans, the news about her origin might put her in a tailspin. Depression was a big possibility.

The touch of her lips on his burned inside him. He could feel her warmth, her embrace, the smell of her. He didn't want the feeling to go away, but it would fade and then he'd just have the memory.

The sun rolled behind a cloud, and the blue sky suddenly darkened. The weather often changed that fast here in the Northwest. Steven made his way down from the observation deck. It was out of his hands now. It had *always* been out of his hands. God was in control. How many times had Courtney said that? And she believed it with her whole being. He'd never seen such a determined, positive person. Her upbeat spirit lifted him each day, and now she wasn't here and he was going to have to come up with his own method of survival.

As Steven made his way back to his car parked in the economy lot, he pondered over his new situation. Two months ago he'd been rattling along with his life as it always had been. Grams had taught him the work ethic. He used to be happiest after putting in a ten-hour day. There was always something new to learn about computers, and Steven learned it well. He was high in demand already, after just his first full year of owning his own business.

He slipped behind the wheel of the Ford, knowing a car would be his next purchase. His closet held new clothes, his refrigerator was at least half full, he had fantastic art prints and one original. Now for the wheels. Courtney liked the old car. "It has character," she'd said more than once. "Wait and be sure you get a good deal. Read the ads, Steven. Something will come up. Probably a little old widow selling her husband's prized possession after his death. We had our Sunday car and then Dad's work car, and later I got the hand-me-down car."

Strange how so much of Courtney had woven into his life. His every thought was of her and something she had said or done.

He opened the day planner before starting the car. The soup kitchen was coming up this Saturday. Of course she wouldn't be back then. He'd offered again to work. There was a question mark in the margin. Did he want to coach the Boys' Club basketball team? There was a need and since he liked the game and had played in school, he knew he could. But could he take the time? It was an unanswered question.

As he merged onto I-5, he thought of God and the verses that had become special of late. "Surely I am with you," from Matthew 28, kept going through his mind. "Yes, Lord, I realize You are with me, but why did You bring this person into my life, then turn it upside down by this burning desire of hers?" Yet even as Steven mouthed the prayer, he knew he would not have fallen so hard for Courtney if she'd been any other way. Fluff she was not. She cared about real concerns. She wanted to make the world a better place. She was kind. Gentle-hearted. Grams would have loved her to death. At that thought he almost rear-ended the car ahead, whose driver was talking on a cellular phone.

"Better keep my mind on the business at hand," Steven muttered aloud. "It's going to be a long two weeks."

Jeff looked up when he entered the office. He had two large rooms filled with old computers and parts. Jeff was good. He just needed direction.

"Hey, man, you better get to work. That new video place over on Morrison just called. Just wanted to remind you about their system being down."

"Oh, no, forgot about them. What'd you tell them?"

"That you were gone for the morning."

"I'll get over there later. Right now I have to—"

"Send out invoices," Jeff finished the sentence.

"Oh, man, I forgot."

Jeff left to answer a call. "See you whenever."

Steven nodded as he looked at the stack of invoices. He was glad he'd be busy this day. He was hoping for a complex problem, something to take his mind from his loneliness. And if it was bad now, what would it be like two and three days from now? That's when the plan began formulating.

He thumbed through the stack of papers on his desk. He needed a secretary. Maybe he should look into that—the sooner the better. He didn't like this part of owning your business. He was one of the best computer consultants in Portland, but that didn't mean that people paid him on time or that their checks didn't bounce. He needed to get the invoices out if he was to have money coming in.

But his mind couldn't get off Courtney. Her eyes were mesmerizing to him, taking over his every waking moment. He tapped the pencil on his desk. At first he'd considered that this might not be love, but whatever it was, he was definitely caught up in the moment.

He leaned back, propping his feet on the desk. "Unchained Melody" played on the little radio Jeff always had on. He would have turned it off, but the melody took him back to another year and another girl, one he'd almost fallen in love with. But Grams had said, "Finish college first, Steven; then think about the girls."

And so he had. He'd graduated summa cum laude, only Grams wasn't there to congratulate him. Nor was his real father, who couldn't be found for any reason.

At three o'clock he had the invoices ready to mail and he headed for the video store.

The system was down, really down. As Steven began testing, he lost track of time and soon it was past five and he hadn't eaten.

"Mr. Spencer?" Becky, the company receptionist, peered around the corner. "Would you like me to bring you something to eat? We have a great restaurant right next door. Their soup of the day is minestrone with beef. I can bring it here, or you could go over with me. I was just getting ready to have dinner myself."

It was irregular, but he agreed to go. He was hungry, having skipped breakfast in order to get Courtney to the airport an hour ahead of time. He followed Becky out the door.

The small café, a mom-and-pop type, had lots of soups and he picked a potato, cheddar cheese, and bacon chowder, along with their house specialty rolls.

He sipped his coffee, then looked up to find Becky smiling at him.

"Do you always get so intense when you work?"

Steven shrugged. "Don't you?"

"Not hardly."

Her smile was nice, and she had a soft look that made him think of Courtney. "I like my work. I love a challenge."

She stirred cream into her coffee. "I can tell."

The waitress brought his soup and Becky's salad.

"I know this may sound weird, but I was wondering if you'd go somewhere with me tonight."

He nearly choked on his first spoonful of soup.

"I guess there is someone, then?"

Steven found it difficult to look her in the eye now. "There is. I'm engaged."

The conversation shifted to noncommittal-type things such as weather, whether an earthquake would hit in the next year, and so on.

"Let that be a lesson," Steven told himself later as he headed back to the office after the problem had been fixed. "Realize that if a woman looks at you with a smile, it might be a come-on." He laughed. Courtney would have thought the whole thing amusing. She probably didn't have a jealous bone in her body. He had been mortified at first, but then felt somewhat flattered.

Jeff looked up from a computer he had torn into and smiled. "That call turned out to be simple. She didn't know how to turn the computer on. Man, you get all the good jobs. I get stuck here with the phone and walk-ins."

"Next time you can take all the calls," Steven said. "Yeah, that's a good idea."

❧

It was after seven when Steven left the office and headed across the river. No way could he go to his apartment tonight. He had to get out and do something. Quite by habit, he later realized, his car headed toward Parkrose and Courtney's house.

Alice was just cleaning up the dinner dishes when she answered his knock. "Steven! What a pleasant surprise!"

He grinned as he entered the familiar house. "Seems my car wouldn't go in any other direction."

They both laughed. "I've already eaten, but there's leftovers. Some chicken and potato salad. If I'd known you were coming, I'd have waited to eat."

He waved her away. "Already ate, but thanks."

"Did Courtney get off okay?"

He nodded. "On time, too. Miracle of miracles."

"You understand why I couldn't go?"

"Yeah, I think so."

"How about a cup of coffee?"

"Yeah, sounds good."

As they sat at the kitchen table, they talked of Courtney.

"She's going to come away brokenhearted, I just feel it."

Steven nodded. "I've been worried about that, also." He reached across the table to cover her hand with his. "She has to do it. She'll never forget about it. God must want her to know. I think her prayers will be answered, and she will find her birth mother. It's just a matter of when."

Alice kept stirring her coffee, though there was no sugar or cream added. "It's difficult for anyone to understand who has never gone through it, but I love her as if I had borne her. She was so tiny and, after one look, I knew this was my child. I'd love her till death."

"Most adoptions are that way, I've heard."

"I used to worry she would one day want to find her mother, that she'd forget about us—Carl and me—but later I knew Courtney would never leave us. The bond between the three of us was tight. And God has been present every second of Courtney's life. I've never believed anything more."

"I know." Steven put the cup down. "I miss her so much. I guess my job is to keep super busy while she's gone. I'd like to take you out for dinner one night and maybe a movie?"

Alice wiped away tears that trickled down her cheek. "You know you already have become a son to me, the son I never had but wanted. I can't tell you how much it has meant to have you come into our lives. And, yes, I would certainly like to do both whenever you can work it into your schedule." She smiled. "You're the one who has a schedule. Me? I'm flexible."

Steven was glad later that he'd gone. Both were missing Courtney. Both loved her to the depths. And together they could be unified and pray that she have her heart's desire.

He didn't tell Alice about his plans, mainly because he wasn't sure when he'd go. He'd wait a few days. Jeff would get his wish and get the house and business calls. He could get a temp to answer the phone. Then he thought of Alice. Why not? She would probably enjoy working for a few days. She could answer the phone and check the appointment book. He'd ask her when he saw her at church on Sunday.

❧

Alice couldn't have been happier to have Steven drop in. He was such a nice boy. He reminded her of her brother, who had died at a young age, before he married. She hadn't thought about Anthony in years. If only he'd lived, Courtney would have probably had cousins. Or if Agnes had been able to have children, there would have been cousins. If Courtney's life had been fuller, maybe she wouldn't have had this urge, yet Alice knew that wasn't the only reason. Courtney felt the need to discover her medical background before marrying Steven and having children of her own. But what if she discovered a terrible disease? What if her father was a criminal? Would that affect her in an adverse way?

Alice checked all the doors and windows, making sure everything was locked up. The fear she always felt at being alone consumed her, and she broke out into a sweat. She wished she didn't have this fear, but ever since she could remember, she'd been afraid once night fell. She picked up her tatting. It was an old sewing project and she hadn't worked on it for years, but for some reason the tiny stitches comforted her now. That and God's presence and the fact that Steven was helping to fill the void left by her loss of Carl, her husband of nearly thirty years.

That night Alice's prayers were as fervent as always, but they were filled with praise. Praise to her God for answering most of her prayers and for giving her such a full, wonderful life.

"Some people never have it this good, God," she said as tears slipped from her eyes. "I thank You for Your goodness to me all these years. And if it pleases Thee, please be with Courtney and help her in this quest. Amen."

The moonlight shone through the bedroom window and Alice forgot her fear. For the first time in a long while she was alone in the big old house, but she felt God's presence there and she knew she never had been alone and never would be again.

twelve

Courtney made her way down the aisle to find her seat, stopping to wait for passengers to place luggage in the overhead bins. She finally got to Row 16 and discovered she had an aisle seat. Across from her was the older lady she'd noticed at the airport being hugged by a young woman with dark eyes.

"Now, Mama, don't be afraid," Courtney had overheard. "You got here in one piece and will return just fine."

Courtney had shivered without knowing why. She'd had eye contact with the two for a brief moment before Steven put his arm around her. There was just something about the young woman's smile and the older woman's face.

Courtney leaned back and closed her eyes. She hadn't slept a wink last night and had hoped to catch a nap once they were in the air. She'd brought a book, her journal, and a poem she'd started a few months ago, but knew she probably wouldn't do anything. She always had good intentions, but she couldn't concentrate. It was more interesting to watch others on the plane.

She thought again of Steven and his insistence on staying until she was in the air. Knowing him, he had stayed until the plane was but a speck in the sky. She felt his presence now, the way his arms felt around her, the touch of his lips on hers. God had been so good to bring Steven into her life. And he was patient. So far he was willing to wait, to hold off the wedding until she found answers about her past. What if the answers weren't here? What if she discovered something terrible? A serious health defect in her family? What then? Would Steven consider marrying and adopting? Yet even as she thought it, she knew what Tina would say.

"How do you know what the background might be of a child you'd adopt? Seems you'd have the same worry, my friend."

Courtney hadn't seen Tina much lately. Large in the final trimester of her pregnancy, Tina preferred staying close to home. Then, too, Steven took up every spare moment Courtney had.

Steven. What a wonderful person. And Bob. He wasn't ready to give up, that much was apparent from yesterday's conversation.

"I don't care how you feel about this Steven; I'm not out of the running, nor am I about to give up," he had said.

"I'm wearing a ring, Bob. That's pretty conclusive," Courtney had responded as she shuffled papers on the desk, wanting the moment to pass. She hated confrontations and Bob was definitely a confrontational type person. *Most lawyers are,* she'd decided.

"People change their minds."

Courtney wanted marriage. Alice wanted marriage. Tina was praying it would work out. And Aunt Agnes. She couldn't forget dear Aunt Agnes. Bob was the only one who opposed it and that was understandable.

She'd packed light for the trip. Most towns had Laundromats, and she wanted to take her one suitcase aboard the plane. She'd heard far too many tales about lost luggage that was never recovered.

A rental car would be waiting for her at Lambert, and

then she'd drive east, across the Mississippi River, over into Illinois, then to the small town where supposedly her mother had lived and borne her.

Courtney had notes and names and a list of towns in the general vicinity. *I'll start with Belleville, then work my way east to the various townships.*

A voice interrupted her thoughts. "Are you going on a fun trip, my dear?" the older lady asked, leaning forward.

"It's business."

Courtney looked at the lady sandwiched between two men who were apparently on business since they were both tapping away on laptops. Something about the woman made her remember how frightened of flying Alice was. Just like this stranger. She could reassure her and even pray for her. She couldn't help it that she wanted to help others. It was just the way she was. It was one thing Steven said he loved about her.

When the flight attendant came down the aisle, Courtney asked if the lady could sit next to her since the middle seat was vacant.

She smiled. "Sure, why not?"

"I'm so glad you thought of this," her new friend said, buckling in. "I'm Dorcas Whitfield."

"I'm Courtney." She extended her hand. "Glad to meet you."

"That's a beautiful ring, my dear."

Courtney smiled. "I'm engaged to a man in Portland."

"And he didn't accompany you?"

Courtney sighed, remembering the endless conversations. "He wanted to come, but it's a trip I must make alone."

"Sounds pretty mysterious to me."

"Well, Dorcas, it's something I needed to do. And where

are you from?" Courtney asked, wanting to change the subject.

Dorcas smiled. "I reside in Illinois. Clancy, to be exact. My eldest lives in Salem, Oregon. I suppose you know where that is. I'm going home, where my other two children live. I've lived in Clancy almost all my life."

Clancy. Courtney's heart spun. That was the name of one of the towns she was going to. What if she was sitting next to a relative? Wouldn't that be a true God-coincidence?

"I may be going to Clancy, myself."

"You, dear?"

"Yes."

"Clancy's awfully small. If you're going for a visit, I'd know the person. I know everyone there. Small-town stuff, you know." Her blue eyes twinkled. "Tell me the name."

Courtney hesitated. *Should I tell Dorcas?* she wondered. *What harm will it do? And possibly some good could come from it.*

"Actually, I do not have a definite name. I thought I did, but the name I searched for on the Internet brought me no results, so now I am studying a definite year and will try to find out about what happened in 1976."

" '76. The bicentennial year?"

Courtney smiled. "Yes. One and the same. It's the year I was born."

"And what are you looking for, exactly?"

"My birth mother." There; it was out. She hadn't wanted to talk about it, but perhaps this would be an answer to her lengthy search.

"Birth mother," the lady repeated. She leaned toward Courtney. "You want to find your birth mother?"

"Yes. I have no idea what her name is because we figure

there is a false name on the birth certificate. My parents adopted me when I was two weeks old."

"Oh, my, oh, my. That's a tough one." She frowned as if trying to remember what happened in 1976. "I don't believe there were any girls expecting then, at least not unmarried ones. And I assume your birth mother was not married, or she wouldn't have wanted to give you up."

It hit Courtney then, a possibility she'd never, ever considered. Perhaps her parents *were* married, but could not keep her. What, then? Didn't responsible people still give up children they knew they could not raise?

"Honey, you come to my house when you hit Clancy. In fact, you can ride with me and my son. There should be plenty of room."

Courtney smiled. "Thanks, but I have a rental car waiting."

"Oh, of course. Everyone reserves everything these days. I'm so far behind; feel like I should be on the Pony Express, not a plane."

The "Fasten Seat Belt" sign went on, and Dorcas suddenly blanched.

"This is my absolute most dreaded part of the trip. I told Sonny I wanted to take the train, but he said, 'No, Mama, the plane is faster and safer.' "

Courtney took her hand and closed her eyes. "I'll say a prayer for a safe landing, Dorcas."

"Oh, child, you do that." Dorcas refused to open her eyes, nor would she look out the window. The wheels came down with a heavy thud and Dorcas squeezed tighter.

"It's okay. We're here. We've landed."

Dorcas opened her eyes and let go of Courtney's hand. "Thank God for yet another miracle."

As passengers made their way up the walkway into the

airport, people waved and rushed forward. Courtney felt the lump in her throat again as she missed Steven. When she went home, back to Portland, he'd definitely be there. And she'd rush into his arms and probably cry like the woman ahead of her was doing. Oh, to be loved. It was surely God's greatest gift to man.

Courtney saw her seatmate grab the hand of a tall, dark-eyed man, and then she was introduced.

"This young girl prayed for your silly ol' mama. Her name's Courtney, and she's going to come see me in Clancy."

Courtney detected a slight frown, then Sonny nodded. "Of course, Mama. You found another stray, did you?" He turned and smiled at Courtney. "No offense, ma'am."

Smiling back, Courtney answered, "No offense taken. I'll be most grateful for a friend in town."

"And you must come for an authentic southern dinner."

"Southern?"

"Of course. You'll be in southern Illinois, you know. We do things the southern way, honey, not like those northerners do."

Courtney hadn't realized, had not dreamed, that there would be a cultural difference between the north and south part of Illinois. If her mother knew this the two short years they lived here, she had never mentioned it.

She took the card Dorcas handed over, promising she'd call the minute she hit town.

It took forever, but at last Courtney had her car, a spiffy red Chevy, and was headed east. A map lay open on the seat beside her. The air-conditioning was on. It was hot, a muggy kind of hot she wasn't used to.

When she crossed a bridge over into Illinois, she realized

this had to be the Mississippi. The river was not at all what she'd expected. After the clear, green-blue of the Columbia and Willamette Rivers, she thought the mighty Mississippi would be even larger and possibly more green. A thin brown stream wove under the bridge she crossed. The land seemed flat, and she wondered where the mountains were.

"Steven," she said, thinking of him for the fiftieth time that day. "I wish you were here. Maybe I should have let you come after all."

thirteen

Courtney pulled off the road into a small rest area for people like her who had to study a map. She was thankful Alice wasn't along. She'd be scared to stop like this. Courtney checked the locks. She was safe.

She opened up the map and studied it. Already she was tired and looking for a motel. It had been a long trip, and she had hardly slept last night. Okawville had her favorite motel, but she didn't want to go that far. Besides, it was out of the way. Belleville was the county seat, and she'd start her search there first thing in the morning.

There were so many villes. Everything ended in "ville." And the towns were small, according to her map.

Folding it up as she knew Steven would, precise and with the folds in the right place, Courtney laughed. *Funny I should think of that now,* she thought. *But when don't I think about him? Is this going to work? What if I miss him too much? What if I can't find anything?*

She looked at the address on the card Dorcas had given her. Suddenly she couldn't wait to see her again, couldn't wait for a friendly face. Courtney wasn't scared, as Alice would have been, but she was lonely. Dreadfully lonely.

With the car air-conditioner turned off, heat poured into the car. It was hot, different from cool, moderate Oregon. She grabbed a tissue from her purse and dabbed at the perspiration on her forehead.

Courtney started the car and signaled to get back on the

road. Such a flat area; already Courtney missed the green-forested hills, the sight of Mount Hood on a clear summer day. She'd drive by Scott Air Force Base where her father had been stationed. She planned to take photos to show her mother, who hadn't been back to the area since they left when Courtney was three months old.

A motel on the outskirts of Belleville with a café next door looked nice and handy. She'd get dinner, call Steven at ten, then relax. She trembled at the thought of talking to him. She missed him more than she'd ever thought possible, and she had left Portland just nine hours earlier.

Landers, Landers, Landers went through her mind as she unloaded her suitcase and overnight bag. Alice said the young girl's name was Landers. The first thing she'd do was look at a phone book.

No Landers were listed in Belleville or any of the other nearby towns. Landers couldn't be spelled any other way. Janelle Landers was the name on the birth certificate.

Courtney changed her clothes and put on a pair of tan slacks and a short-sleeved yellow cotton sweater. Thank goodness she'd included some cooler clothes. Her mother had been right.

The café was small but adequate. Courtney studied the menu, ordering a Cobb salad with extra bacon and a roll. That'd do her.

She read the local newspaper while she toyed with the avocado. It wasn't fun to eat alone. Maybe she wouldn't wait until ten to call Steven. She needed to talk to him now.

The girl bagged up the remaining salad and took Courtney's money.

She went back to the motel with M&Ms, the leftover salad, a newspaper, and a local advertising circular. It listed houses for sale and rent; she wondered what it cost to live here in Belleville, Illinois.

The room was stuffy because she hadn't left the air-conditioner on. It was going to take some time to get used to the weather here.

Steven answered on the first ring. "Honey. Courtney, are you okay? Was the flight all right?"

A warm spot inside her expanded. How she wanted to be with him this very moment, put her head against his chest. "Everything's fine, Steven. I'm fine. And you?"

"Missing you."

"Ditto."

"Dropped by your mother's—"

"Already?"

"She was more than glad to see me."

"Well, of course. I told her to stay with Aunt Agnes, but she didn't want to."

"I love you," Steven said huskily. "I just know these next two weeks are going to take forever."

"Maybe I'll find my mother tomorrow."

"And if you do, you'll want to stay and visit. Catch up on family things. Meet your cousins and so on."

"If and when I find her."

They talked about a concert he had tickets for in November and the soup kitchen, which she'd miss.

"I'll tell Gerta hello for you."

"And don't listen to her ramblings."

"Oh? That I am the luckiest guy in Portland to have found my true love?" He chuckled. "No; I think I can handle that."

Courtney hung up with Steven's closing words in her ear. "Good-bye, my sweet love."

Was she making a mistake? Did it really matter what her mother might have had or what medical horror her ancestors had? Steven would marry her anyway. He'd said so more than once. And if they had a child with an affliction, he said they'd love it anyway. Maybe more so.

She turned the TV on and back off just as fast. In the silence of the room, she curled into a ball on the bed and sat staring into space. An image of what her mother might have looked like burned bright in her mind. Always she was pretty with blond hair. A round shape. Her smile would tell Courtney how much she was loved and how much she hadn't wanted to give her away.

Laying her notes out on the bed, she studied the map again. The search at the courthouse could take most of the day. The historical society was also a good place to begin as well as the library.

She'd wait a day, then call on Dorcas. She'd been so kind, though she'd acted a bit strange when Courtney mentioned the year 1976.

The next morning seemed cooler as Courtney, dressed in jeans and a red blouse, headed over to the café for breakfast. She had parted her hair, pulled it back, and put a large barrette in the back.

She hoped she didn't look too much like a stranger. She had an idea this place was almost like Clancy, where everyone knew everyone else.

After two cups of coffee, scrambled eggs, and an English muffin, she packed up her notes and headed out. She'd stay at the motel tonight, then decide if she wanted to stay in another town.

As she headed into Belleville, she wondered how old her birth mother was, if she knew the Lord at all, and also if she had not wanted to give up her child. If not, why did she? Courtney could not imagine in a hundred thousand years giving up her own flesh and blood, and she knew Alice would have been behind her 100 percent, urging her to keep her baby. They were like that. Not all parents were supportive, though.

What if she'd run away? But where would she have gone? If none of the relatives would take her, she'd have had to stay in some small rundown room and work nights and leave the baby with a sitter. No, probably her mother had traveled the only road she could.

The midday sun beat out of the sky when Courtney descended the courthouse steps. Dead end. No Landers. They said a child hadn't been born in the county on July 8, 1976. No births recorded. Period.

It was lunchtime, but she couldn't think about food. Not now, not when she knew she had so much to do and possibly not enough time. Maybe she should have brought Alice. Alice could have searched in books and looked on microfiches. Yet Courtney knew her mother would fidget and act all nervous. It was better this way.

The library was small and smelled of old books. Courtney loved the smell of books, newspaper, and new leather. She took a deep breath and walked up to the main desk.

"No computers for our users' help," the plump, dark-haired lady said. "All we have is the old card catalogue. We're looking to be computerized by mid-2000." The librarian smiled. "Is there something I can help you with?"

Courtney explained part of her mission and the librarian looked interested. "I'd suggest looking through newspapers. The newspaper morgue is in the basement."

Courtney spent the rest of the afternoon going through

the 1976 papers. A lot had happened in 1976. It seemed every town had a celebration of some sort, and some had small parades to commemorate the Bicentennial. What a year to be born!

Still no Landers. There were two births registered the day before and one birth the day after July 4, but nothing for the seventh, eighth, or ninth. Courtney jotted down the names, adding them to her long list of possibles.

"We're closing," a voice said at her elbow. "Perhaps you can come back tomorrow?"

"Oh." Courtney jumped. "I didn't realize it was so late."

She hurried up the stairs, thanking the librarian, who was closing up the desk.

"Do come back, dear. And if I can help in any way, let me know."

"Dead end," Courtney muttered as she went to her car. "This is impossible." She wondered then if Dorcas might have some ideas of how and what to look for next. If her mother had registered under a false name, she'd never find her. How could she?

The evening breeze felt good on her skin. The library was air-conditioned, the basement almost clammy. She liked seeing sunshine, hearing cars, and seeing people walking. She was in civilization again.

The car was warm as she headed toward Scott Air Force Base. A guard stood at the gate, asking her mission.

"You don't know anyone here? You have no ID card or reason for coming on base?"

She shook her head.

"Ma'am, I hate to tell you this," he leaned down and looked at her skeptically, "but we don't issue passes to just anybody. You must have a sponsor before I can let you on.

Do you know anyone stationed here?"

"Heavens!" Courtney cut him off. "I don't need to go on the base if it's going to create a problem. I was just curious." She held her camera up. "I'd take a few photos for my mother. My father was stationed here in the mid-seventies."

"I'm sorry, but that's not a good enough reason."

"I understand. No problem." Courtney waved, then turned the car around. She'd get a photo of the gate with the name on the sign. That would have to do.

She headed back to the motel and to the café. Maybe she'd try a chicken-fried steak tonight. And mashed potatoes with cream gravy.

The café was busier tonight, and a Garth Brooks tune belted out from the jukebox. Something about, "This is your song."

The steak was okay, but she couldn't eat all of it. Again she took a doggie box to add to the one from the previous night. She'd dump them out when she left in the morning.

Because it was too early to call Steven, she decided to take a drive through the countryside. She passed through one, two, then another town. Strange, but nobody seemed to be outside, nor were any of the businesses open except the local taverns on the corner. It was nothing like the hustle and bustle of Portland. Finally she turned and made her way back.

Steven answered before she heard the ring.

"Honey, you're late!"

"I am?" She glanced at her watch. "It's just nine-thirty."

"I wanted you to call me at seven our time."

"Oh, right."

"I've been a basket case today."

"You have? But, why?"

"Nothing's gone right. Jeff finally figured out the configuration on this program."

"I'm sorry."

"When did you say you were coming home?"

It was not a good conversation, and she felt guilty for leaving. She looked at the ring on her finger. It reminded her of a better time coming, of hope for the future, of Steven's love. His words had not helped.

"Call me in the morning," he finally said. "I know what the arrangement was, but I need to hear from you twice a day, not just once. Call at nine your time."

Courtney promised she would, then hung up, her heart aching. How could she go on like this? Not eating right. Her mind always thinking of Steven. Maybe something would happen tomorrow.

She flipped on the TV and half watched *ER* while she did the word search in the newspaper.

fourteen

Dorcas was happy to hear Courtney's voice and gave her explicit directions to her home. "You'll be here for dinner, then?" she asked.

"What time?" Courtney asked.

"No later than six, honey. Is that okay with you?"

"Oh, yes. Sounds fine," Courtney answered.

"And you feel free to come at any time, you hear?"

Clancy, similar to the other towns in the area, was small with one main street of businesses. A funeral home with stucco falling off, three taverns, a Methodist church, a Catholic church with a high steeple that tolled the hour with loud chimes, a grocery store, and a small drugstore were the extent of it. George Washington Grade School was in the middle of town, and a small park with a baseball diamond was at the far end. A new settlement of homes was north of Main Street. Courtney headed out there and drove down the blocks, where small saplings were planted in each yard. Children played in the street, but moved as she drove slowly past. Of course they stared. People knew she didn't belong here.

She headed back out of the housing area and back through town. She dug out Dorcas's address—12 Birch Street. She'd passed Birch already. It was in the old part of town. She decided not to stop just yet.

The midday sun had given way to late afternoon heat as Courtney drove out of town and headed to the next one.

Cornfields dotted the landscape. What she wouldn't give for a small soft drink. Maybe she should buy a cheap ice chest and just carry cold drinks in the car. She'd never imagined it would be this hot the end of September. The grass was brown, and the birches back in town were shedding leaves.

Five miles later she came to Breese. Funny names for towns. Probably family names. She stopped at a drugstore and asked if there was anyone named Landers living nearby.

"Landers?" The tall, buxom lady shook her head. "Child, I'd know if any Landers ever lived here. Lived here all my life, never been any farther south than Mascouta nor more north than Renton."

"You haven't been to St. Louis?"

"What do I need that big town for?"

Courtney smiled and paid for the local newspaper and a package of gum.

It was past lunchtime, almost dinnertime, and she needed food.

She went back inside and asked where she might eat.

"Go on up to Renton. They got two cafés there, honey. Here you have to go to the tavern and they do make the best fried chicken of anyone I know, but then I don't know many people outside of this here area."

Courtney thanked her and hurried to her car. Fried chicken sounded really good, but she figured Dorcas would cook that for tonight.

It was now hot, a scorching heat, and Courtney thought it was because there were no trees to lend shade, at least not once you were out on the main drag. She missed the tall firs from home. The only kind she had seen here were short and scrawny looking, although there had been a few oaks in the middle of town.

What do people do for entertainment? she wondered. So far she hadn't even spotted a theater or a bowling alley. In Belleville there were both, but not here. Not in the small towns. It would be strange living in such isolation.

She found a small café and ordered a chili dog and fries. She observed the locals laughing and joking, but nobody paid any attention to her. It was as if she were invisible.

She drove back to Clancy and pulled up in front of a tall, narrow house set amongst a grove of trees. It was painted mauve and had a burgundy trim. A fence surrounded the house, and a gate was unlocked. Courtney held her breath as she ventured up a sidewalk that had obviously recently been replaced. The grass was brown and thin in spots, but a few shrubs were blooming under the bay windows.

She hesitated, then pressed the old-fashioned buzzer.

The door swung open and Dorcas threw her arms open. "My little Courtney! I'm so glad you came."

Dorcas had a pot of tea brewing and a plate of hors d'oeuvres waiting. She chuckled as Courtney came in and looked around.

"You didn't expect a refined home in a Victorian setting, now did you? Not here in farm country."

Courtney hugged the older lady and glanced at her surroundings. Large photos in oval frames decorated one wall. Wainscoting was throughout the living and dining room. A settee was in one corner with a Duncan Phyfe table and end tables.

"It's just too beautiful," Courtney exclaimed, clasping her hands. "I feel as if I'm walking into a room from *House Beautiful*."

Dorcas chuckled. "I consider it a compliment. Now come, let's have a cup of tea, then I'll show you the rest of the house. Sonny can't make it for dinner, so it'll just be the two of us, but that's okay. That man keeps way too busy, if you ask me."

"A workaholic," Courtney said. "My father was that way, too."

Courtney sipped the tea and smiled. "Very good. And I like the smells coming from the kitchen."

"You may find the guest bedroom especially interesting," Dorcas said. "Let's go now." She led the way up a long flight of stairs with a highly polished banister. "And, yes, you may slide down the banister, if you so desire."

Courtney laughed. "Were you reading my mind?"

"Perhaps."

"Please excuse the dust," Dorcas said, running her finger along the floorboards. "I used to have a maid do all of this, back in the days when I entertained. We had a book club going and a tennis club. Mr. J., my husband, never liked to entertain, so I just had women come in. Once when I mentioned the DAR, they almost ran me out of town."

Courtney chuckled. She couldn't quite imagine the scenario and found it difficult to believe that this was Rebel country. Not that she didn't have empathy for those who fought so hard for the South. After studying both sides of history, she felt the South had just cause for their grieving. But, that was a subject she usually avoided.

"This is the room where I want you to stay, should you choose to stay overnight in Clancy."

"It's wonderful!" Courtney clasped her hands, falling in love with the guest bedroom with its high ceiling, wainscoting, and huge four-poster bed with flowered canopy dominating the center of the room. A fireplace took up the west wall.

"This used to be a sitting room, but I decided to use it as a full-fledged bedroom, and the offer is open to stay for as long as you'd like."

"Oh, my, no, I couldn't do that," Courtney gasped. "It's so very kind of you, but it would be an imposition, though you might say not."

Dorcas walked over to a photo on the armoire. "Here. I want you to look at this picture."

The frame was exquisite, with curlycues and an angel with wings in one corner. She looked at the eyes staring back at her. "Is this someone who fought in the Civil War?" The suit looked military. But it was the bold look, the piercing stare of the eyes, that shook her.

Dorcas cleared her throat. "Now you will accept my offer. Now you will understand."

"Understand?" A chill raced up Courtney's spine. "What do you mean?"

"If I'm not mistaken, the man you are staring at is your great-great grandfather, and he fought in the Spanish American War of 1898."

Courtney nearly dropped the picture. "But—how—what—I don't understand—"

"It's a long story. Come sit in the next room while I tell you about it," she said.

"Jeremy Johnson, the man in the photo, was my grandfather. He had gone to Texas, then up North, and ended up fighting in that war. When he came home to Massachusetts, he married into the prosperous Eddy family. My father was his eldest child and after my mother died of TB, my father left Massachusetts and came here. Why he landed here, I'll never know. I was a young girl of sixteen and soon met and married my husband, God rest his soul.

It was a happy marriage; we had four children."

"But, how—"

Dorcas leaned forward and took Courtney's hand. "I'm getting to that part, and it will help you, but not in what you really came to find out."

Courtney started to open her mouth but closed it again as Dorcas continued.

"Our eldest son was born with a hole in his heart. Money was no problem as I had funds set up in a trust by my grandparents, and Jonathan's father owned half of this county."

"And your son is my father and you're my grandmother?" Courtney had started to piece it together.

Dorcas held her hand up. "Don't get ahead of the story, my dear. There's much to tell."

"Jonathan Jr. went to some of the best hospitals in the land. Johns Hopkins was one, and I know you've heard about the wonderful work and research they do. Our son had an operation, back when it was just an experimental type thing.

"He came home," Dorcas went on, "and started living a normal life."

"Normal, meaning he went to school and stuff like that?" Courtney interrupted.

"Yes. More than anything he wanted to play basketball, being tall and lean, but the doctors said no, he could not."

Dorcas removed a small white handkerchief edged in lace and dabbed at her eyes. "He was such a smart, but stubborn, boy. He was probably my favorite, being sick and all. Mothers have a way of favoring a firstborn and especially one who is ill."

"He died, didn't he?"

Dorcas nodded. "Yes, my dear, he did. When he was nineteen."

"I'm so sorry. But how do I fit into this picture?"

"A month after his death we received a letter from the Watt family. They lived two towns over. Perhaps you've been to Darby?"

"No, I haven't—but I searched the records for the entire county and found nothing."

"That's because you're asking for Landers and it isn't Landers that you want to know about, but Watt."

Leaning forward, Courtney gasped, "You mean I'm part of the Watt family?"

Dorcas nodded. "Yes, you are. So, it was providence that put us on the plane together. Do you believe in fate?"

Courtney shivered. "I believe that God allows certain things to happen and this must be one of them."

"Our son disobeyed and played basketball at the gym when we didn't know about it. It was there he became good friends with Miller Watt. Miller, a wild boy, had a sister with an affliction we later learned was epilepsy."

Courtney cried out, "No, I don't know if I can bear to hear all of this. Not yet."

"You're right. This is too much to assimilate all at once. I debated about bringing it up, but you seemed so desperate to find your family. But, let's go downstairs and have some more tea. I'll let this sink in before going further."

Tears rolled down Courtney's cheeks, and she couldn't stop them. She was an illegitimate child, though Pastor had said there were no illegitimate children, only illegitimate parents. Still, her parents had not married, since one was rich and the other from the wrong side of the track. And her mother had had epilepsy?

For certain she could not hope to marry Steven now. How could she, knowing this? How could she risk having a child with that disease? She'd been spared, as the tests had ruled out epilepsy, but it probably had just skipped a generation, which often happens.

Dorcas was fussing around in the kitchen, and Courtney sat huddled in the large Chesterfield chair. Its long arms and seat seemed to enfold her, holding her close. Suddenly she wanted Steven here with her, and her mother. Alice would know what to say and do. Alice would assess the situation and ask more questions, but Courtney was too numb to even think straight. It was far more than she could assemble at once.

She refused the tray of appetizers and held the teacup so hard she feared it might break.

"I cannot be absolutely certain, child, that you're my granddaughter, but the facts indicate this."

"My mother was definitely a Watt then, not a Landers?"

Dorcas nodded. "That part of the picture is the hurting part, Courtney."

"But I must know! I have to know!"

"Sherry Watt was such a cute little thing. All eyes and a big smile. She was in the same grade as my Jill. They weren't friends, but in a small school and area, everyone knows everyone else. The Watts lived in an old rundown house at the edge of Darby. Her father didn't own any land around here; just worked for others. He was dishonest from all I've ever heard about him. I'm sorry about this part, but his daughter Sherry was smart. Cute as a button. I think she had another name, but I can't remember it just now. I hired her one summer to clean house and wash windows."

"Do I look like her at all?"

Dorcas smiled. "Perhaps your build more than anything, but I see my son's eyes in you. I had that feeling sitting next to you but didn't know why or how it could possibly be. I had to think about it before telling you this. Surely you understand my reasoning."

"What happened to my mother?"

"Her father put another name on the birth certificate, I heard, so she could never be traced. I'm sure it was all her father's doings. He was mean and ugly, if I do say so myself. Everyone stayed clear of him then."

"So that's why I couldn't find any record of it."

"I'm sure Emil would make sure it was a false birth certificate. He may have falsified the date as well. He knew how to take care of things."

"What happened after I was born?"

"They moved in '79, I believe it was."

"And went where?" She had to know.

"Not sure, honey. When Sherry had you, the family insisted she give you up for adoption. They were barely making ends meet as it was. And they knew she'd have a crazy child." Dorcas shook her head. "They were superstitious. Not sure where that came from, but they thought she was crazy; they didn't accept the doctor's explanation about the epilepsy being controlled with medication."

The knot in Courtney's stomach grew until it clutched her so hard she could hardly get her breath.

"I think we shouldn't go on. You are positively pea green."

Courtney began sobbing, and once the avalanche started, she couldn't hold the tears back.

Dorcas was there, holding her to her bosom, rocking her gently as one does a child. Courtney was her grandchild.

She didn't care how she'd come to be; the important thing was that she was hers and she had loved her from that first moment. Yes, God had answered her long-ago prayer to know what had become of her son's only child. She'd lain many sleepless nights, regretting that she hadn't done more, hadn't searched for her grandbaby.

"Did my father love my mother?" Courtney choked out. She had to know.

Dorcas brushed the hair back from damp cheeks. "Darling, I know he did. I saw the romance unfold before my eyes and should have done something to nip it in the bud, but I didn't. We wanted him to go to college—he was behind, of course, as the illness had kept him out of school for weeks at a time. We tutored him, but still held him back a year."

"If he loved my mother, that's all that matters," Courtney said, her heart suddenly swelling with the love she felt for Steven. "I was a love child, at least."

Dorcas nodded, loving Courtney for her gentle smile and her loving, tender manner. "I know you're right, child."

"But," Courtney pulled back, "I still must find my mother."

"It's not going to happen, honey, but I've said enough."

"You don't think I can find her because they moved? But now I have the proper name and someone can help me."

"Perhaps so. I wish I could help more. They left the old house—it's still out on the main highway about nine miles from here. They moved on when it was condemned."

"You mean you don't know where they went?" It was too much; she convulsed into sobs again. "But I must find her."

Dorcas wished she had some answers, but she didn't, and Courtney's pain became her own.

"Honey, I want to call your adoptive mother. She needs

to be with you now. Or your fiancé?"

At the thought of Steven, Courtney's head shot up. "Oh, no, I couldn't let him know. I have to break my engagement."

"But, why ever, dear?"

"Because of my past, my family, the people I came from."

"If he loves you, that is not going to matter one whit. Your family are the dear people who adopted you and taught you and loved you and made you who you are now."

Courtney believed that; she'd always been told that, but something hurt so deep inside, she didn't know how she could marry. Not now. Probably not Steven. It would take time to heal.

"As you already said, if God didn't want you to discover this, He wouldn't have made sure we were on the same plane, sitting next to each other. He wouldn't have led Steven to your church; He wouldn't have given you such loving, supportive parents."

Courtney glanced up. "I think I want my mother, Alice, to come. She may not fly; she is fearful of planes."

"That's fine. She can take a bus and come right here to Clancy, believe it or not."

Courtney dialed the phone number and waited for her mother to answer. The answering machine clicked on after the fourth ring.

"Mom, it's me, Courtney. I want you to come. I need you." She recited the number. "I've found my father, at least."

As she replaced the receiver, the tears began again. She'd found one link to her heritage, and she was so grateful. Finding her father was wonderful, and to think that Dorcas was related—but what about her mother? Her mother was more important—or was she?

fifteen

Alice came home from a full day of learning her part-time, eight-hour-a-day job exhausted. Never, even in the early days of marriage, had she worked more than part-time. Her volunteer work was six-hour days, but that was different. She could leave at any time. Still, she was happy to do it—happy to help Steven out and happy to have her mind on something besides Courtney.

She went straight to the refrigerator and opened a can of 7-Up. Sinking into the recliner, she took a long sip, then turned on the news. Every bone ached, yet it was a good feeling. If she could just stop worrying about Courtney. She'd always been a worrier; Carl had chided her about it more than once, and later Courtney scolded her. She'd had an uneasy feeling about Courtney all day, not knowing why.

Alice closed her eyes and listened to the latest weather report. She knew she would drift off before finishing the soda, but that was okay. There was nobody to cook dinner for. Nobody to entertain. Her last thought was that she was glad Steven had asked her to take over as receptionist for the five days he planned on being gone to be with Courtney. She would have liked to be with her child, but it was more important that Steven go now.

It was a surprise when he'd said he'd booked a flight out that weekend. "I just have to do this, Alice. She may not understand; she might be miffed at first, but I'm praying she'll be happy I'm there."

"And I'm sure she will."

❧

The doorbell wakened her suddenly. It was Steven, his face filled with anguish. "I'm leaving earlier than expected, Alice."

"What's wrong?" Panic seized her. "It's my baby. What's happened to Courtney?"

"She wants you to come, and maybe you should, but I want to be there with her and I—" His face was white.

"Sit, Steven. Relax. Tell me what this is all about." Alice had always been good in emergencies. All that time when Courtney was ill and they hadn't known what was wrong, hadn't known if she'd ever completely recover, Carl had come apart, but she'd been the stalwart, calm one. Of course, God had been her mainstay—not that Carl didn't believe, but he hadn't been able to let go and let God take over. She was now being pressed into service again.

"I can make coffee. Or tea."

Steven shook his head. "I couldn't swallow anything right now.

"She called you, you know."

"She *did?*"

"Did you listen to your messages?"

Alice gasped. "I didn't even check. I was so tired and thirsty; I just went straight to my favorite chair."

"That's fine. I think that's the way it was meant to be. When she didn't find you home, she called my voice mail and I got the message just a few minutes ago."

"What happened?" Alice grabbed his arm, fearful of what she might hear.

"She's found her father's family."

"Her father's? What about her mother's?"

"She wasn't clear on that point, but whatever, she's deeply upset, and I'm flying out first thing in the morning. Couldn't get a flight out tonight; they're all booked up. Some business convention in St. Louis."

"And you want me to go?"

"If you want, Alice. I can shut down the shop or just put on the answering machine and let Jeff handle the most important calls." Steven paced the length of the living room and back again. "She didn't ask for me. She wants you, but I must go, and you do what you think best."

"She wants me to come?"

"Go listen to your machine."

Alice played the message back and heard a frantic voice, so unlike Courtney, who always was in control of everything. Even in her illness, she'd been brave, certain she would be okay. And she had been. But this was something new. Different. Something she had no control over. And she had asked for Alice. Not her fiancé, but her mother. And if Carl had been here, she would have asked him to come, too.

She listened to the message twice, her hand gripping Steven's.

"I can't fly, Steven. I have such terrible fear of flying. If I go, it would have to be by bus. And it would take two days at least. She needs someone *now*." She put her hand on his shoulder and then he had his arms around her, hugging her hard.

"I'm going. Maybe you should come, too, even if it is by bus."

"Steven, I'll be more help if I stay and answer the phones for you. I learned all I needed to today. Just knowing that Courtney wants me to come means more than words can say."

"I'm sure Courtney will understand."

Alice nodded. "She knows my fear of flying. She'll understand, all right."

After Steven left, Alice replayed the message. This wasn't Courtney's voice at all. She sounded so—shattered. Her baby was frightened.

Alice went to the sewing room at the top of the stairs and pulled the trunk out. She lifted the lid.

Inside was the scrapbook she'd kept from the moment Courtney came to them. There were albums, too, but this particular scrapbook contained all the baby congratulation cards, then the early birthday cards.

The baby book was another treasure. She would never have not kept a record of all of her precious baby's doings.

"What if someone comes to take her away from you?" her sister Agnes had asked once, before Courtney's first birthday. "You know that happens."

"I'll fight them for her."

"Would you, Alice? I think not."

They had been fortunate that that hadn't happened, and soon they relaxed, knowing that Courtney would always be their child.

Alice removed the first pair of tiny shoes, the gold locket with a photo inside of Mommy and Daddy, the christening dress and the white lacy bonnet. She'd kept everything, preserving them in a large plastic bag. Someday Courtney might want them for her child.

Courtney had loved looking at her special clothes and her baby book. There was the locket of hair in a small envelope; her first haircut, it said on the envelope. There was a photo of her taking her first steps in the Mary Jane shoes.

She had taken ballet at age four, and Alice remembered

the tutus she wore and the recitals for two years. She was always the shortest and the most clumsy. But it hadn't mattered.

Courtney had always asked about her real mother and father, wondering if she looked like them.

Alice opened the baby book. Had Courtney's mother wanted her? Had she loved her while carrying her? Somehow Alice thought so, since Courtney seemed so content as an infant, and there were facts now stating a mother's feelings mattered while she carried her child.

She held out her favorite photo, taken when Courtney was six and just starting school; her hair was in long curls, her smile wholesome. "My little pixie," Alice murmured. "I love you, my little pixie."

❧

Steven left, driving like a maniac back across town, praying all the while that Courtney would understand, that she would talk to him once he got there. A fear deep inside made him think otherwise, and he so hoped his gut feeling was wrong. . . .

He packed light. Even if he stayed five days, he could wash his clothes somewhere. He didn't want to take the time to check his baggage or have to wait there for it to come down the baggage chute.

He'd called ahead and would have a car waiting, a small compact. If only it weren't so far to Clancy, where she was staying.

Courtney was in pain. Steven knew her well enough to realize that. She would never have called asking for Alice to come if not. Nor would she have called him on the pager unless she was desperate. This was her problem and she'd find the solution, she'd said more than once in the days before leaving for Illinois. Why hadn't she at least given him a clue? He had nothing to go on, only guesses, and what if she didn't want to see him? He had to take his chances. He loved her. He knew God had brought them together—thanks to Grams—and he wasn't going to bow out now. It didn't matter what she found out; they'd weather it together—stand united. Wasn't that what it said in the Bible? Apostle Paul's words came to him, but he couldn't remember from where. It was something about it not being good for man to live alone. Steven, not always filled with such determination, would fight this one. He'd fight to the end, if need be. Courtney belonged to him, and he didn't care about her background. They'd fight it together.

Sleep wouldn't come; he knew it wouldn't, so he tried to get interested in the late-night movie. It didn't work. Nor did the latest Grisham novel grab him. Music filled the background, soft listening music so he wouldn't bother the other tenants, though he thought the building was well insulated.

Finally he relied on a few passages from the Good Book. He'd marked them earlier after a discussion with the pastor. They calmed him down as he finally drifted off, only to hear the alarm ring at five.

Jeff had been only too happy to drive him to the airport. He let him off at the entrance. "Take it easy, man. You'll have a coronary if you get any more riled."

"Take care of the little guys, too, not just the corporations," was Steven's parting shot. "Do what you can, but get some sleep and food, also."

"Hey, man, I'll be okay. This is my chance to prove myself."

The car roared off and Steven rushed down the aisle toward Gate 18. He had to go through the metal detector booth, but that was quick. Two pairs of pants, two shirts, and two of everything else was all he carried on.

Once he was on the plane, Steven got comfortable, hoping to catch up on some shut-eye once they were in the air.

You are doing the right thing, a voice seemed to say as he buckled in.

"Grams, is that you?" he said aloud.

"Were you speaking to me?" a voice said on his right.

"Oh, no, just talking to my Grams," Steven said.

The man's eyes widened. That took care of that. No small chitchat now. The man thought he was crazy, for sure. What if he'd said he was having a conversation with God? What might have happened then?

Steven's dreams were of Courtney, the white dress she'd wear down the aisle, the candle they'd light together, indicating the life they'd share, the promise to serve God, to let Him be head of their household, then the kiss after the minister said, "I now pronounce you man and wife." And then the wedding night when Courtney would be his, only his. Then the children they'd have.

The attendant's voice wakened him. "Sir, do you want a cola or a cup of coffee?"

"Coffee. Yes. With cream and sugar, both."

He never used cream and sugar, but this occasion called for it.

"You looked pleased," the man to his right said. "You were smiling. Must have had a good conversation with Grams."

Steven leaned forward, letting his seat snap back to an upright position. "You don't know the half of it."

Over coffee, the two men chatted, and Steven was glad he had talked to the man. It made the flight seem shorter, and he'd made a friend, in spite of his talking to his grandmother.

He had a rental car waiting, but it took forever to find the car rental place, then way too long to sign his name. *What was the point of calling ahead with the necessary info?* he wondered.

With a map at his side, he drove out of the airport and toward Illinois. With luck, he'd be there by one. He didn't have this Dorcas's address, but in small towns, someone would know. He'd ask at the first business establishment he came to.

As he hummed along with a gospel song on the radio, his heart jumped in anticipation of seeing Courtney again, of being able to comfort her, to reassure her that he was with her no matter what and always would be.

sixteen

Courtney slept fitfully that night. The bedroom was wonderful. It was the sort of room she would have hoped for in a bed-and-breakfast. The feather bed—she'd never slept in such a thing before—seemed to swallow her in its soft depths. She could have stayed here forever—here where her needs would be met, where she didn't have to think about what had happened in the past.

She'd also never slept in a canopy bed before, and it made her feel like a princess. Long, lacy curtains hung on all sides, offering semi-privacy, considering one could see through the lace. She didn't like them closed; it made her feel too hemmed in.

It was too warm for a fire, but she longed for flames to mesmerize her, to take her away from the discovery of the evening before.

As morning's rays splashed across the bed, the sunbeams dancing, Courtney grabbed her robe and pushed her feet into slippers.

She walked across the room and picked up the photograph. Her great-great-grandfather's eyes—if indeed her birth story were true—bored into her very soul. God had been good to bring Dorcas into her life. She belonged to someone now. She should be content knowing that much, but it was what she didn't know that had kept her awake most of the night.

How would she find her mother since she'd moved away? And how about other relatives? She must learn more about her mother, more about her physical condition. Would anyone even want to talk to her should she find them? Would they deny she was part of them? She'd heard of that happening. She couldn't understand why, but birth mothers often didn't want to be found. Oregon had passed a law saying the records should be open for all to see, but four birth mothers had filed appeals against that law, and so far the records remained sealed, just as they did in most other states.

Courtney wondered why Alice hadn't called back. Had she not been home? Had she gone out to stay with Agnes? She should have called Aunt Agnes instead of Steven. Steven wouldn't understand the turmoil she felt now. She loved him so much, but how could she expect him to understand. How could he possibly want to marry her now?

She lay back on the bed, burying her face into the soft folds of the comforter.

A large leather-bound Bible sat on the small nightstand. She hadn't noticed it before and wondered if Dorcas had slipped it into the room while Courtney soaked in the huge clawfoot bathtub last night. The tub was huge, big enough to hold two people, and her thoughts returned to Steven and what it would be like to be married to him. *Enough of those thoughts,* she'd chided herself. It wasn't meant to be.

The smell of coffee drifted up the stairs. Of course Dorcas would be up early. The morning sun had already heated up the house. There were no mountains or high hills to offer shade. No clouds to cover it. It would be a blazing, hot day. After breakfast she would call Aunt Agnes and see if her mother was there.

"Good morning, Courtney!" Dorcas called out, turning from the stove and coming over to hug her guest. "My, don't you look pink-cheeked this morning. You must have slept well in the feather bed."

"It's heavenly."

"Sit. I'm making pancakes from sourdough starter a cousin brought me from Alaska, oh, about twenty years ago now."

"The same starter?"

"Oh, my yes. And it makes the best, most tender pancakes you've ever sunk a fork into."

"I need to call my aunt Agnes. She might know why Mother didn't answer my call last night. They'd discussed Mom going out there. Both are widows now."

"That's a good idea, but why not eat first?"

Dorcas didn't tell Courtney about the call she'd received that morning—Steven calling from the airport, saying he was on his way, but to please not tell his fiancée.

Dorcas gave her a choice of bananas or grapefruit to eat first. Courtney chose the bananas and soon finished the fresh, sliced bananas topped with real whipped cream. Then Courtney ate four pancakes, immersing them with Dorcas's homemade syrup that was good and full of maple flavor.

The kitchen was large and airy as morning light filled the room and Courtney's heart. Today was going to be special. Perhaps her mother was already on her way. Perhaps she had pushed aside her fear of flying and would arrive sometime that afternoon.

Dorcas tried to detain her, but she had things to do, places to go. Soon Courtney was in the red rental, zooming down the long driveway back toward town.

She talked to the lady who ran the small gift shop. Dorcas had said she might have some information.

"And you're who?" The pleasant-faced woman seemed guarded. "I don't give out information to just anybody."

Courtney had to relate the entire story for what seemed like the hundredth time. "I really need to find my mother, so if you know anything about the Watt family, I'd be ever so grateful." She also told her about staying with Dorcas, but did not mention that Dorcas was probably her real grandmother.

"I knew Mrs. Watt. I knew her kids, but they took off and nobody has heard from them since. Unless—" A thoughtful look crossed the wide face.

"Unless?" Courtney didn't like prompting people. "Unless what?"

"There was a cousin. One twice-removed, I believe. A cousin from the mother's side."

"And?"

"She lives over in Darby."

"Darby?" Courtney knew that would be her next stop for sure now.

The lady pointed east. "It's the township ten miles over. You'll go through Reese first."

"Do you have her name?"

"No, can't say that I do. She married, of course, and the only thing I know is Lois. Yes, Lois was her given name."

"Oh, thank you, thank you so much."

Finally, she'd found something to follow up on. Racing to her car, she heard a horn honk and figured someone thought she was racing across the street in front of them. She stopped when the horn blasted again as a voice called her name. She paused, her heart pounding as she recognized the voice. But it couldn't be. Steven had a business to run. He wouldn't have come all this way in hopes of finding her.

But he had.

He stood, leaning against a small white compact, waiting to see what she would do.

"Steven?" And then she ran across the street and into his arms. The tears began and he held her tight, smoothing the hair back from the sides of her face, saying nothing. Sometimes words weren't necessary. Touch was more important. Presence was also important. Words would come later.

"I missed you so terribly," he finally said when the sobs had ceased. She now had the hiccups, so he held her arm up as Grams used to do when he got hiccups. That made her laugh as she looked at him through her tears.

"But, why did you come?"

"Did you really expect me to stay away?"

The sun shone on his face and Courtney felt the fierce longing she always felt when she looked at him.

"I guess I expected you to honor my request."

"You called Alice."

"She's my mother, Steven, and I suddenly realized how much she means to me and this whole quest and I just needed to see her."

"But not me."

"I didn't say that—"

"No, not exactly."

"So you're here because?"

"Because I wanted to come. Because you need me. Because I care about you. Because you are part of me. Because Alice doesn't like to fly. But mostly because I love you."

She broke away and looked into his deep, craggy face. "Oh, Steven, I can't marry you now. I just can't. Not after the things I'm finding out."

"We'll discuss it over a cup of coffee. I see that little café is open."

"I have to get to Darby."

"I'll go with you."

"You can't." The smile left her face and his heart nearly stopped.

"Why not?"

"As I said before, I must do this on my own."

He took her hand, but she pulled away.

"Steven, I just can't think about marriage. I can't even discuss it now. It's not good that you came."

"You didn't feel that way a minute ago."

"I know. I was so—well—relieved to see you."

"And you love me."

"Yes."

"Then I want to go. Isn't that what love is about? Isn't that what God intended? That we share one another's burdens—make them lighter? I don't understand why you don't understand that concept, Courtney." His voice sounded hard.

"Steven, I'm sorry you spent that money and came all this way for nothing."

"Nothing is for nothing. I'll never believe that."

She turned, walking away from him. "I don't expect you to understand."

"And I don't. That's for sure. I won't let you go, if that's what you're thinking. I won't give up. I'm not one to run home and to give the ball back. I will fight this, Courtney. I don't care about who had you, what they were like, what medical problem they had, if they were in prison. None of that matters. Not one bit!" His voice had risen and a person across the street stared.

"Shh—" She put her hand on his lips.

"I won't hush. You can't make me. You go ahead to where it is you're going and I'll just follow you in my little rental car. I'll follow you today. Tomorrow. And the next day and the next."

Courtney squeezed her eyes tight. She couldn't cry again. Not here. Not now. Not on Main Street in town. Not in front of Steven. There had already been too many tears. She couldn't succumb to them again.

"Come on. Let's discuss this inside the car. Yours or mine?"

She said nothing, but followed him back across the street, slipping into the seat and watching as he made sure she was safely in before closing the door. The warm, soft interior made her suddenly laugh, the first time since she'd left Portland.

"What?" He looked puzzled, as if he couldn't believe she'd be going from tears to laughter.

"It's rare that you hold the door open for me, considering you can't even open the passenger door on the Ford."

"You're right. It felt good, now, didn't it?"

She smiled. "Very good. I'm sorry, Steven, for acting like this, but I feel strongly about it, and you just have to understand."

"I'm trying. Believe me, Courtney, I'm trying."

"You need to head east, since you're so insistent. But you're staying in the car, should I find this Lois, who may just be my cousin."

"Will do."

And he meant it. He didn't care what the conditions might be. As long as he could be there for her, to lift her up, to pray with her, to cry with her, or to rejoice. It didn't matter. God had not put her into his life to suddenly snatch her away. He'd never been more sure of anything in his entire life. And with a self-confident smile, he put the key in the ignition and headed out onto the street, going in an easterly direction.

seventeen

In a matter of minutes, Courtney filled Steven in on her father and how her mother had worked at the Whitfield home.

"She was just a maid, Steven. And she fell for my father. Of course he couldn't marry her. He was ill, too. We could have a child with a hole in its heart."

"What is Dorcas like?"

"She's wonderful, Steven. She wants to see me again and would like to meet you."

"She called me, you know."

"No, I didn't know."

"It's probably just as well."

The afternoon had cooled off as a gentle breeze blew in from the west.

"Shall I shut off the air-conditioning?" Steven asked, noticing Courtney's hair flying in the breeze. She'd opened the window after he'd started the car.

"Yes. I much prefer the fresh air, even if it smells like corn and harvesting and cows and things."

He laughed. "It does smell different than the exhaust fumes in Portland, yes. Kind of nice for a change. Brings back memories of Redmond and home and the ranch."

Courtney looked thoughtful. "It must be wonderful to know exactly where you are from and who your mother was, and even though she died, you know who you are. Oh, Steven, I don't know why I'm doing this." Her mood shifted. "I'm so scared of what else I'll find."

"I know, honey. I know."

"But, do you?"

"Well, I think I do." His hand reached over to cover hers. "I know nobody can know unless they've gone through it. I never knew my parents, but at least I knew who they were, faults and all."

"That's just it. Not knowing and wanting to know, yet afraid to find out. Afraid of rejection. Of not being loved."

"You'll always be loved by those who know you and consider you their own flesh and blood. You know that, honey. Nobody could love you any more than Alice."

At the thought of her mother, the woman who had nurtured her all these years, tears came to her eyes again. "I'm tired of crying, Steven. I refuse to cry anymore."

"Then don't." He slipped an arm around the back of the seat. "I think we should sing some praise songs. Won't that help?"

"Yes!" She belted out one of her favorites, her voice drifting off into the winds as they tootled down the highway:

"Heavenly Sunshine, Heavenly Sunshine!
Filling my soul with Glory divine,
Heavenly Sunshine, Heavenly Sunshine,
Jesus is mine!"

"I don't know that one," Steven said after she'd sung three choruses.

"I learned it before I knew how to talk yet. It's always been a favorite on a day when the sun is shining. We don't sing it much anymore. Maybe I'll request it at a Sunday night service."

"I like it, too. Sing it again."

And so she did, her voice even higher and louder than before.

"Praising God makes me feel better. Why did I let myself get so worked up?"

"It's understandable."

"I still can't marry you, though. I need to think about this. There's just too much going on."

Steven's face dropped as he turned away, not wanting to say the words that had popped into his mind. Patience. God was teaching him patience in many things, this being the most important right now.

"I was hoping we could set a date. Alice is eager to start planning a wedding." Steven looked straight ahead. "Could we maybe discuss that possibility?"

A town loomed up and he slowed to twenty-five.

"I need time to sort this all out. You said before that you understood."

"I'm trying, really, I am, Courtney."

"There's something sinister in my background. I can't just ignore it."

"Sinister?"

"Yes; my grandfather was not a nice man."

"In what way?"

"He lied to my parents, for one thing." And then she was telling him about how her folks had paid for hospitalization and for Sherry to get on her feet.

"I probably have the same in mine. We can't all be perfect." But even as he said the words, Steven felt a sinking sensation. She wasn't going to let this go. Maybe never. Maybe Courtney wasn't the right one for him after all. If so, there surely would be some indication. Some sign. Maybe he'd been wrong in coming here. Yes, she did need time and he had interfered, blundering in where and when he wasn't wanted. He should have insisted that Alice come, even if it was by train or bus.

"Background is important," she said.

Steven didn't reply.

"I am sorry, but you can at least talk to me."

"I guess everything's been said, Courtney. I shouldn't have come. I see no recourse but to leave on the first flight I can get out of St. Louis." He stopped the car and turned it around. "I'll take you back to your car."

"But we're almost there."

His jaw was taut. "No, it's better this way. You're absolutely right. I should never have come. You didn't ask me to. I just thought. . ." His voice drifted off.

"Steven, don't be angry with me." She looked at him expectantly, but he still stared straight ahead.

The five-mile ride back was soon over and he pulled up behind her car. She glanced over, but he wouldn't look at her.

Her mouth went tight. "Maybe you want this back then." She twisted the ring off her finger and put it on the seat beside him, then yanked the door open. Without a backward glance, Steven backed up and made a U-turn and headed west. He didn't even kiss her good-bye. He wasn't able to trust himself to do just that, not when he wanted so much more, something he now doubted he could ever have.

Courtney stomped over to her car and flung the door open. "Let him be that way. It's better that I know now than later." She slid into the seat of her small red car, wishing she had called Steven back, wishing now she had told him she needed him and wanted him here with her, but she couldn't do it. She thought of the alexandrite. Why had she given it back? That was the end of the end. Now Steven was angry, or was it a hurt reaction? She didn't blame him. Her mood swings were unbelievable. One minute singing praises to God, the next fear and doubt. Yes, most of all doubt. Doubt about a future that might not be hers to enjoy.

The scenery was the same, the weather the same, but a chill raced over her as she knew she couldn't have done it any differently. How could she marry Steven knowing what she did about her family? No-account people. A grandfather who was mean and not liked by any of the people in town. He'd made her mother work. He'd probably made her give up her baby. He couldn't have known God and could not have reared Courtney right. She knew she should be thankful for Alice and Carl, for the love they'd bestowed on her, the home she'd always had. How different things might have been. Yet, could she turn her back on her family should she find them? Perhaps they needed to know God. Perhaps they would listen to her. She'd never know until she found them, until she discovered who and what they were.

She passed through Reese and saw the next town was five miles east. Of course. All the townships were five miles apart, no matter which direction they went.

Courtney had to pull over once because she couldn't see through her tears. *How silly of me,* she admonished herself. *I got exactly what I asked for*. And it was true. All her life she'd known what she wanted and gotten what she wanted. Sometimes it happened instantaneously. Sometimes it didn't. When the illness struck, she'd prayed for healing. Her parents had prayed for healing and the entire church prayed that the doctors would be guided into finding the right answers. She'd had to wait. She'd learned patience in that six-month period. Like her birth father, she'd been tutored and had kept up with her class. She'd later graduated salutatorian. Yes, God had given her a decisive mind, apparently unlike her mother. From what she'd heard thus far, she was more like her father's side.

She pulled back onto the road. Such light traffic. It was a treat to drive down the highway from small town to small town. An occasional car passed. Those who did come along wanted to go much faster than her fifty-five.

She tried to swallow the hard knot in her throat. Why had she not taken her ring back? Why hadn't she asked for it? She really should never have taken it off. She loved Steven with her whole being. She knew she did. He had to understand. He'd agreed with her plans in the beginning. But he'd wanted to orchestrate; he'd been insistent on coming, and when she said no, he ended up coming anyway. But Alice hadn't, and that was the tender side of him that had come, that had wanted to be with her and that had left his business to come to be with her. So it seemed he really didn't understand after all.

Another car beeped and drove past her, a car full of teenagers in a hurry. "Hey, lady, why don't you get a horse?" came the call. One kid made an obscene gesture, and Courtney felt sudden fear. She was out where nobody could help her should someone decide to pull her over. Her body could be tossed so easily in the cornfields. The harvest was over, but the stalks stood tall and, though dry and brown, held their own.

She clicked on the radio, searching for a Christian radio station. She must get her mind off of such gruesome thoughts.

Darby came into view. A couple of buildings stood in haphazard fashion, leaning toward the ground. A small grocery store and a post office were on the right. A café with a peeling sign was directly across the street. Courtney pulled into the post office lot. The postmaster might know someone named Lois. It was worth a try.

"Lois? No last name?" The woman smiled. She was the postmistress of the small town. "Pretty hard without a last name. I know of two. Lois Johnson and Lois Oberthauff. What age would she be?"

"I think older. Maybe twenty years older than me. Someone in their mid-forties."

She nodded. "That'd be Oberthauff then. She's out of town about half a mile. Turn at the first road out of town and go left. The road dead ends at their house."

"Oh, thank you. And wait—I want to send these post-cards. I need stamps."

Courtney dug out the cards she'd picked up earlier for Tina, Steven, and her mother. She'd send Steven's even though she'd seen him. The knot came back.

She thought about getting a quick bite to eat, but the place didn't appeal to her, though she'd discovered that often the smallest places had the best food. She knew she wouldn't be able to swallow anyway. It was just that way.

Courtney followed the directions and traveled extra slow on the potholed dirt road. She imagined it would be hard come winter if they had rains like the rains back home.

The farmhouse was old, but well kept. The lawn was green and trimmed with a huge hydrangea bush in full bloom at one side. A row of bright yellow marigolds bordered a front flower bed.

The house painted white with red trim made her remember

how the Cape Cod at home had once had red shutters like this. Awnings were on the left side of the house, shading it from the sun's rays in the evening. The right side also had awnings.

Courtney pulled into the far side of the U-shaped drive.

A door opened before she got out of the car and a robust woman came down the steps.

"Hello. You lost, miss?"

Courtney held her handbag tight, walking toward the woman. "I think not. The postmistress in Darby directed me to your home."

"Oh. How can I help you then? I don't recognize you at all. . . ."

Courtney stood in front of the woman, searching her for some sign of similarity. The high cheekbones? Shape of face? Color of hair?

"I'm Courtney Adams. I have reason to believe you might know my birth mother."

The woman's face blanched as if she'd seen a ghost. "Your birth mother?" she repeated.

"Yes. I have papers to show you and conversations to discuss. I really need to find my mother for medical reasons. I hope you can help."

"Come on in. I'll put on some water. We have an hour before Mel comes in for his meal. He's a bear if I don't get it on the table at the dot of twelve."

"I understand."

The house was well kept and picture-perfect inside. Crisp curtains fluttered at the windows. Western furniture upholstered in bold blue plaid dominated the room. A Western painting dominated the wall up over the fireplace mantel. "The Heartache's on Me" by the Dixie Chicks sang from a radio, probably in the kitchen.

"This is a lovely room," Courtney said.

"Well, sit while I bring us something to drink. Coffee or tea?"

"Coffee, please. No sugar or cream."

She took a deep breath, trying to decipher if the woman knew anything. She was hospitable, kind, as many were toward strangers, but had there been recognition, a glimpse of something in those eyes?

"Now, tell me who you are and exactly what you think you know and what led you here."

Courtney began from what she knew about her birth, the adoption in Belleville, her parents moving back to Oregon, the desire to find out her background after the illness, and meeting Dorcas on the plane and finding out who was probably her father.

"I see why you are interested in finding your roots. It can be very beneficial in some cases." Lois stirred her coffee vigorously. "I may be able to help, but I'm not sure I want to."

"What!" Courtney suddenly jumped up, nearly spilling her coffee. "How can you say this?"

Lois sighed. "There is no concrete proof, for one thing, so why give you info that could be wrong?"

"But I want to know anything. Maybe I'm grasping at straws, but that's better than knowing nothing." Courtney sat back down. Outbursts were uncalled for and so unlike her. Just as tears were.

"Your mother may be my first cousin. Our mothers were sisters."

"Oh, Lois, I need to know where she is. I want to talk to her just once; even on the phone is fine. I just have to know something about her. If you have a photo maybe—"

"I have one photo. That may sound strange, but our families were not into taking pictures. My aunt Bernice married a no-good-account poor farmer. Emil knew nothing about farming or making a living. He—well, no need to go into all that just now."

"But I need to know everything. Please, oh, please." Her eyes welled up with tears again. "My mother, your aunt?"

"Courtney, I'd let you see your mother, but it's quite impossible."

"Is she living in Europe? Australia? Where?"

Lois stood then and walked over to the window, looking out. "Your mama loved you. You need to know that."

Courtney's heart jumped. "I was loved? I heard that the house was condemned and that my family moved on. I'm hoping you know where."

"Yes, the place was condemned and is barely standing." Lois paused, as if searching for the right words. "You were born in my husband's mother's house."

"Oh, my." Getting closer gave Courtney a heady feeling. "I thank you so much and if I could come back after lunchtime, that's fine. Right now I'd just like to walk around on the grounds where my mother once lived and played."

"And died."

"Died?" Courtney could never explain the sinking sensation she felt at hearing the news that she would now never see her mother face-to-face. Never would there be a hug, a kiss, an exchange of facts over the years. No declarations of love. How could she stand it?

eighteen

"How—did she die?"

Lois looked away, tears filling her eyes. "Your mother died three years after you were born, three years after her beloved baby—you—were taken from her arms."

"She didn't want to give me up?"

"Not hardly. She loved you more than life. If you only knew how many lovely things she made before you were born. Lacy little sacques, nightgowns, a crocheted bonnet with pink ribbons—"

"I have one of the nightgowns with pink crocheting." Courtney swallowed hard, thinking of her mother painstakingly making such beautiful things for her.

"She knew you'd be a girl. She saved some of the money she made from keeping house for the Whitfields and had my mother buy flannel so she could make a blanket. We bought the flannel in Belleville. She hid everything, not wanting to rile Uncle Emil any further. She also hoped her father might change his mind, might let her keep you, but he was afraid you would have the same affliction and he couldn't stand to have another 'crazy' in his house."

"A 'crazy'?" She shivered. Wasn't that what Dorcas had said, too?

"He was very superstitious and thought she had the devil in her. Many a times she was beaten. It was because of this she started going out with boys, boys she knew would never marry her, but would love her, even if only for an hour." Lois hesitated. "You have no idea how much this hurts to tell you, how I've kept it inside me all these years. The only pretty part of the picture was the fact that a childless couple adopted Vannah's child and gave her a good home—"

"Vannah?" Courtney said the name twice. It had a nice sound, a different sound. Then she remembered Dorcas had called her Sherry. "Maybe we're not talking about the same person. I heard she went by Sherry."

"Oh, that. She lived in a dream world and thought Sherry sounded more romantic. The family called her Vannah, her given name."

"I need to know how she died, all the details, if you don't mind." Courtney looked at her ring finger. The imprint was there as Steven's engagement ring had been on her finger for two months. She had had to give it back. How could she keep something so precious, so wonderful, when she had no right to it? She was just plain, common white trash.

"The important message is that your mother loved you with all her heart and soul. She was forced into giving you up, but believe me, that was far better than the life you would have had under the Watt roof."

"If only I'd known her. The photo you mentioned?"

"It's in my special album upstairs. I'll go fetch it. I also have something else for you."

Courtney set her cup down. The coffee was cold, but it was wet and made it so she could swallow. "I very much want anything my mother had or made."

Courtney waited as doors closed and a shuffling noise ensued. Then the footsteps came back down.

"Here it is." She bent over Courtney while she looked at it. "This is me on the right and my brother on the left. Your mother, shorter than us, is in the middle."

Courtney held the photo as a combination of joy and love welled up inside her. Her birth mother. What a nice smile. She felt her own mouth. Yes, she had her mother's mouth. Very definitely.

"You look some like her. Same build, and yes, your mouth is the same. But you are so refined by comparison. Happy. With a confident air. All things Vannah never knew in her short life."

Boots stomped outside and Lois jumped up. "I forgot the lunch, but it'll just take a second to microwave the soup. Excuse me."

She looked at the photo again, wondering if Lois had found the other object she'd mentioned. She'd take anything, even a silly drawing from second grade. Voices sounded and Lois tried to appease the deeper voice.

"Not that soup again, Loie. I was hoping for a couple of your thick sandwiches."

"It'll just take a second, Mel."

And then he was in the living room, staring at her. "So? You've come looking for your heritage, have ya?" A short, broad-shouldered man looked at her out of intense brown eyes. Courtney felt a fear rush over her and grasped the sides of her chair.

She stood. "I'm Courtney Adams and my mother was—"

"I know who your mother was. I knew about you, too."

"Mel, the sandwiches are ready," Lois called out.

"I'll be there in a minute." He strode over in stocking feet and touched her chin. "You look like your mother. Very much so."

"You knew her, too?"

"Of course. Everyone knows everyone in Darby. My dad bought this land from the Shermans, who had rented it to your grandpa."

Courtney's head spun. It was all so confusing. How could she ever keep things straightened out?

"We used to run around. Your mother's brother, me, Lois, and a few other kids." He looked serious. "That was a long time ago now. Nobody knew for the longest time that Vannah was pregnant. She kept it well hidden."

"Mel, don't you think—"

He waved Lois away. "That's the one thing about being my own boss. My time's my own."

"Yes, but—"

He thumped the table and glared. "Wrap it up. Or, better yet, ask our guest to have lunch with us."

Courtney wished she could just disappear. She sensed hostility between this couple and didn't want to be caught right in the middle of it, nor did she want to be the cause of it. Perhaps she should come back tomorrow.

"I—really should probably go."

"I can meet you at the bakery in town tomorrow morning," Lois said, a bit too anxiously, Courtney thought. "We can talk more and I'll give you the few things I kept. Since we were cousins and all, it was decided I should have her belongings. And one such gift is something I know she'd want you to have."

Courtney hurried out of the farmhouse and down the steps. Yes, meeting at a restaurant was a much better idea. She felt relief, yet fear, and she wasn't sure why. Surely God wouldn't have had her come all this way for nothing.

The blistering sun shone down on her back, making her glad to be in the car and moving again. She thought she saw a face at the curtained window but couldn't be sure.

She drove around until hunger forced her to drop in at a small drive-in in Okawville, the largest town outside of Belleville. She sat in the cool corner of the small café and chewed on French fries. Her search had all but ended. She was free to go home tomorrow. Or the next day. If Lois would just keep in touch. And if she could tell her where she could find other members of her family. This was all so new to her. The idea that she had cousins and maybe aunts and uncles. But her mother was dead. Her dream of being held, being told she was loved, would not come true now. Epileptic. Her mother had been taunted for her disease, made to feel she was unworthy of love. If only Courtney could have seen her just once and told her she loved her, thanked her for giving her up to a loving adoptive couple.

"Ma'am, are you okay?" a voice was at her elbow. "I asked if you wanted anything else."

Courtney looked at the young girl with pimples on her face. "I—no—that is, I am just fine and don't need anything."

"Refill on the soda?"

Courtney nodded. "Yes, a refill would be nice."

She found herself thinking about meeting Lois tomorrow.

❧

Steven drove faster than the speed limit as he headed back toward the city. He'd had enough of farm life. Enough of this countryside, the cornfields, and the searing heat. He couldn't wait to get back to Portland and back to work—so he could forget. Yet a voice made him stop and think.

Patience. All of God's children need to learn patience. It's truly a virtue.

He thumped the steering wheel. Patience be hanged. He'd been more than patient. He'd been loving, waiting, yearning, wanting, and hoping. Yes, above all, hoping that Courtney would find what she was after and that she'd be able to get on with her life—their life—and want them to make a life together. He loved her so very much.

Sometimes you have to let things go, free them.

He'd freed her all right. She wasn't his, perhaps had never been his. Why had it taken him so long to figure it out? Courtney didn't want marriage. Not now. At least not to him. He felt the ring in his jeans pocket. He'd never give it to anyone else, though he hoped God would lead another woman his way—and soon.

An impossible hurt consumed him.

Belleville was out of the way, but he felt the need to go to a larger city, get lost, and think about things. He already knew there'd be no flight to Portland until morning. He called Jeff, who said things were fine. No big problems yet. And Alice was working in the office, handling calls as if she'd been there all the time.

"I'll be back tomorrow, Jeff. Think you can hang on until then?"

"Courtney?"

"Don't ask."

"Okay, man. Just thought you might plan on staying another day or so. We're doing okay. People don't mind waiting. I even helped one lady with a problem over the phone."

"Good for you, Jeff. You get a raise."

There was a chuckle at the other end. "I knew you'd say that."

Steven hung up and pulled into the nearest restaurant. It offered steaks on the billboard and somehow he felt like eating a ten-ounce medium rare. And then he'd find a motel and watch a movie before going to sleep.

But he couldn't get Courtney out of his mind. As he picked at his salad, he missed her so much—wanted her with him. The waitress had a nice, warm smile and gave him the idea she'd be happy to see him when she got off. He might not have thought about it twice, but she mentioned the time her shift ended. He'd never been into picking up women, but the idea got to him now. Maybe he could put Courtney from his mind.

She was waiting outside the restaurant when he left. The night air was balmy, almost sticky.

"Could you give a girl a lift?" she asked.

"Sure. Hop in."

They chatted while he drove the miles to her home. "I suppose you think I sidle up to all the men."

He grinned. "The thought had occurred to me."

"Well, I don't. It's just that you looked so lonely and sad and I don't like to see a nice man like you sad."

"I have reasons."

"You aren't from around here, are you?"

"No. I'm here on business from Portland, Oregon. I go home tomorrow."

"No chance of staying or perhaps coming back?"

He pulled up at the house she'd pointed out.

"No, I doubt I'll ever be back here."

"Just thought I'd ask. No harm in asking, now, is there?"

He waited while she got out of the car and then she leaned over. "I thank you for the ride and the conversation. If you get lonely enough, you know where I live now."

Steven pulled back onto the main road and sighed heavily. He could have had a date. He could have forgotten about Courtney for one night, but something compelled him to move on; a voice seemed to say that this was not right, and he knew it wasn't. Grams would have been mortified. *Give Courtney time,* the voice said. *She just needs time.*

What was the rush, anyway? He'd waited this long without a soul mate; he guessed he could wait a while longer and make sure he found the right one. God would nudge him when he needed to make a move. Even so, he'd never give the ring to anyone else. It was Courtney's ring. It would always be Courtney's ring. Somehow he figured Grams would understand.

nineteen

Courtney, who usually ran late, was right on time, but Lois was already there, leaning against her car. A small box was on the hood. Courtney waved as she hurried over. "You're early."

"Farmers get up early," Lois said with a half smile. "Mel left on a business trip to St. Louis. I have the whole day to relax and talk to you."

Courtney felt exhilarated. "I say let's get some coffee and maybe something to eat."

"I've eaten," Lois said, "but I'll have one of Hilda's cookies. She bakes the best."

The bakery, with a long room extending along the west wall, was nearly vacant. Tim McGraw sang from a small radio perched on a shelf.

They took their coffees and went to the far corner. Courtney ordered a cinnamon roll, lightly warmed, and Lois got a chocolate chip cookie.

Courtney scooted across the booth. "I am so excited about this. I could hardly sleep."

"We're cousins, you know," Lois said. "I never, ever thought this day would come."

Nodding, Courtney looked pleased. "Cousins. You have no idea how good that sounds to me. I've always dreamed of having a cousin."

Lois smiled. "I have lots of cousins but rarely see any of them. Everyone has moved on to greener pastures, as the saying goes."

"I can hardly wait to see what you brought."

Lois's green eyes sparkled. "I don't have much, but what I have is yours."

"Oh!" Courtney was so taken back, she could scarcely speak. "I would be happy to get anything."

Opening the box, Lois handed over a crudely painted picture. "I have no idea why or how I even got this. It was in Vannah's personal belongings, the few things Aunt Bernice didn't keep."

Courtney studied the painting, the kind kids paint in first grade. Her mother loved blue, as there was dark, light, and medium blue splashed across the now-stiff paper. A yellow sun peered out of one corner. A green tree was in the middle with red apples in the branches. A girl sat in a swing, her legs stretched out. She held it up. "Do you think this is supposed to be my mother?"

Lois nodded. "Yes, I'm sure it is. Most kids do self-portraits or family members at that age."

The waitress came with the huge cinnamon roll and several pats of butter. "And here's a carafe of coffee." She smiled at Lois. "How're you guys doing, anyway? Seems I never see you."

"Fine, Kristi, just fine." She turned to Courtney. "This is my long-lost cousin, Courtney."

"Hello." The young woman smiled broader than before. "Pleased to meet you. Are you from around here?"

Courtney shook her head. "Afraid not. I live in Portland, Oregon."

"Oregon!" Her eyes widened. "Goodness, but you're a long way from home."

Lois stirred cream into her coffee. "Yes, she is. In fact—well—I have to look into this, but she might be related to you, also."

"Go on now!"

"I'll let you know after I think about it for a minute," Lois said.

"Are you sure about that?" Courtney asked, suddenly more interested in the young waitress.

"Listen, I declare, everyone is related to someone in this area. We don't have many people moving here and so many stay on, so cousins marry cousins, and what do you know? More cousins."

"First cousins?" Courtney asked.

"Oh, I'm sure not. First cousins can't marry, as you must know."

Courtney buttered her roll and took a small bite. Her heart raced so much she could scarcely swallow. It was almost too much for her to comprehend. Family. How she'd always longed for family besides Aunt Agnes and an uncle she never got to see.

"You're not married?" Lois asked then, glancing at Courtney's now-bare finger.

"I was engaged."

"Was?"

"Yes. We broke up just yesterday, just before I arrived at your house."

Lois set her cup down hard. "You mean he's from around here?"

"Oh, no. He's a native Oregonian and just followed me here."

"He did? Now *that* sounds romantic."

Courtney felt a small tug at her heart. Maybe it sounded romantic, but their parting words had been anything but romantic.

"He doesn't understand my quest."

"Quest?"

"Yes, quest. My mission to find my birth mother."

"Well, you've found her, so what's the problem now?"

Courtney took a long sip of her coffee. "It's just that I cannot marry without knowing my mother's medical background, and I am so hoping you can answer some of my questions."

"Then what?"

"I'll know if I should marry or not."

Lois leaned forward. "My dear cousin, one can always marry, no matter what. Perhaps you should not have children; that's your decision."

"This is true, but I *want* children. Doesn't everyone?"

Lois shrugged. "Mel did not."

"No? And?"

"We've never had any."

Courtney didn't know what to say. She'd just always felt that life wouldn't be complete without having two or three babies.

"So, back to why you must know about your mother's health. Do go on."

Soon Courtney was telling her about the mysterious illness and how she'd had a series of tests with nothing conclusive.

"Did you have seizures?"

Courtney recoiled, remembering that night, just as if it had been yesterday. Waking in a sweat, she'd twisted and turned and soon Alice had been there with cold cloths, wiping her forehead. And then she'd convulsed and minutes later she was wrapped in a heavy blanket and on her way to the emergency room of Woodland Park Hospital.

"I do not have epilepsy. That was ruled out. My convulsion happened because of my sudden rise in fever. The doctor said that was not unusual. It's never happened again and he said probably it won't."

Lois nodded. "Then for sure you do not have epilepsy."

"But what if I'm a carrier and my child is born with it?"

"And what if your child is born with cystic fibrosis? Or with muscular dystrophy or contracts leukemia when he's two years old like my friend's child? Don't you realize everything is a risk? Nobody can be assured, just as you might get hit right out in front of this bakery and die on the spot."

Courtney shivered. "I know, but—"

"No, I don't think you know."

"My mother definitely had epilepsy?"

Lois nodded. "She didn't go to school on a regular basis. She had grand mal seizures. The seizures scared everyone and most of the kids shunned her. It was awful for her."

"And her parents?"

"You probably heard from Dorcas Whitfield that they were superstitious."

"Yes, I did."

"That's why she couldn't keep you." Tears welled in Lois's eyes. "Such stupidity. I cannot imagine carrying a baby for nine months, then being forced to give it up."

"I always wondered how my mother could give me up, or why—"

"Well, wonder no more. She made all those baby things for you, hoping to see you wearing them, hoping that her father would reconsider. Of course he had the final say in everything that went on in that family."

Lois set the drawing aside. "I also have a photo of the family, without Vannah. Who knows where she was."

Courtney studied the faces of the people standing in a yard, a big, old house in the background. Lois pointed to the tallest person. "That's Emil. And George. Miller. Your grandmother Bernice, and the baby, Clyde."

"My mother was the only daughter?"

"Yes, which was just as well. Emil needed boys to work the land, to farm. Vannah could do nothing some days. The least bit of stress caused her to have a seizure."

Hundreds of questions ran through Courtney's mind. There was so much she wanted to know, needed to find out. Her mother had been sickly all her life? What might have happened if she'd gone to a doctor in Chicago or a large city? Someone who specialized in epilepsy?

As if reading her mind, Lois continued, "A doctor was suggested in St. Louis. That's closer than any other large city here in Illinois, but Emil said they couldn't take the time or the entire day lollygagging when nothing could cure the seizures—"

"Not cure, but control," Courtney broke in.

"I know, honey. Believe me, Aunt Bernice did everything she could to try to convince her husband otherwise."

Courtney felt sick suddenly. Perhaps it was the cinnamon roll. Too much, too sweet on an empty stomach, but she knew it was far more than that. "If only he could have been persuaded."

"You might have grown up here? You might have had Emil's hand on your backside not once, but twice a day? Is that the kind of life you are missing now?"

Courtney winced. "I never thought of it like that."

"Well, you should. Emil was a *mean* man. The boys left as soon as they could, when the house was condemned."

"I heard he was mean."

"Yes. The landlord, who turned out to be my father-in-law, didn't want to fix the house up. The only way to get Emil out was to have the county say it wasn't fit to live in. And it did look pretty bad."

"Where was my mother?"

"She died the month before."

Courtney refilled her cup with coffee. This was the part she had to know but wasn't sure she wanted to know now.

"How did my mother die and where was she?"

Lois took a bite of the roll Courtney had pushed to the edge of the table. "I'll just have a taste since you're through."

"Sure, go ahead."

"Vannah must have had a seizure as she was coming downstairs that winter morning. Whatever—she tripped and fell headfirst."

Courtney shut her eyes tight as it soaked into her mind.

"She was dead when the ambulance arrived."

"Dead from the seizure?" Courtney asked.

"I don't know if it was the fall or the seizure. No autopsy was performed. You had to know Emil. The EMT, a friend of Mel's, said she had a broken neck."

Tears slid down Courtney's cheeks and onto the table. "I can't believe something could happen like that. And nobody even cared!"

"Yes, people cared." Lois touched her hand. "Believe me, a lot of people cared about your mother. A lot of us loved her."

"But, why couldn't someone do something?"

"You just didn't cross Emil, nor did you interfere with someone else's business. A schoolteacher tried, back in fifth grade I think it was, and Emil had her fired."

"But he couldn't do that."

"Oh, yes, he could and did. It's not what you know, but who you know, and someone on the school board apparently owed Emil a favor."

Courtney felt the tightness expand in her stomach. It was too unbelievable. "I just wish I could have known her."

"She was gentle, Courtney. And just in case you're wondering, she named you before they took you from her arms."

"She did?"

Lois handed a sheet of paper over. "Here are some scribblings I found in a notebook. She wasn't sure which one to choose, so she wrote down several names. Isn't it strange how she liked names starting with *C?*"

Courtney took the paper and stared. Her name wasn't among the list, but there was Carole. Chastity. Camille. Catherine. Chelsea. Candy. Charlotte. Cynthia. Then one was circled. Cerise.

"Cerise?" Courtney exclaimed. "That's a color. It's deep to purplish red. I think it's French."

"It was your mother's favorite color. They buried her in a dress my mother made special for her. It was cerise with a white lace collar."

"Courtney Cerise," Courtney said aloud. "That's going to be my new middle name. I think it only fitting, don't you?"

"Would you like to go to the cemetery?"

The breath caught in Courtney's throat. "I—never thought of that. Of course I want to."

"And we can drive out by the old house."

"It's still standing?"

"Oh, yes. It's just five miles beyond my place and about three from the cemetery. We'll do the cemetery first.

"I'll give you the diary she kept. You can read it on the plane ride back to Portland."

"I won't be able to wait until then," Courtney said. "I'll read it today. Tonight."

Kristi brought the bill and both hands reached for it. "Let this be my treat to my newfound cousin," Lois said. "If you want, you can buy lunch later."

The sunshine bore out of another clear blue sky as Courtney followed Lois to her car. She'd insisted on driving, since she knew where to go. They made arrangements to leave Courtney's car parked around back in the alley.

"I have to buy flowers," Courtney said then. "A bouquet to put on the grave."

"There are no florists here or in the next town. We farmers just don't buy enough to keep them in business."

"What about the store? We could go and buy a flat of marigolds—"

"Not this time of year, but we can pick some of mine."

And so they did. They were short-stemmed, but the bright orange was beautiful. There was one purple hydrangea left on the bush. "Almost as if God wanted my mother to have her favorite color," Courtney said.

Lois nodded. "It's a nice touch."

They got back into the car. "It's not far. A small plot out at the edge of Darby. If you didn't know to turn, you'd miss it altogether."

"What did my grandmother do when Vannah died?"

"Aunt Bernice went into deep depression, hon, the likes of which I've never seen. She blamed Emil. I know that's why they left the county, and with the house being condemned, there was nothing holding them here."

The cemetery was less than an acre in size and Lois went directly to the plot. There was no headstone, just a marker on the ground.

Courtney fell to her knees. She'd so wanted to meet her mother face-to-face, hold her close, tell her she loved her, and there was no mother, only someone buried in the ground. Someone under this marker with her name and birth and death dates etched lightly on the concrete, twenty-one years ago.

Courtney traced the letters with her fingers: *Vannah Louise Watt, Born March 31, 1960, Died April 5, 1978.* Courtney arranged the small bouquet just right, making a circle around the stone.

"She was eighteen and six days," Lois was saying. "Eighteen and an unhappy, lost soul."

"Did she know God?"

Lois smiled. "Funny that that hasn't come up before. Yes. She did. All the kids attended church and Vannah accepted the Lord as her Savior one Sunday morning a couple of years before she got pregnant with you."

"Thank You, God," Courtney said, realizing she hadn't thanked the Lord for leading her to this cousin, to this small plot in a cemetery that contained the remains of her mother.

"Let's go to the old homestead," Lois suggested.

Courtney got up from the grave, brushing dried grass from her knees. "Yes, I'd like that very much."

The house, once tall and magnificent, was a weather-beaten gray as if it had never seen a coat of paint. Windows were broken out. Rotting steps led up to a porch that ran along the entire front of the house. It, too, was caving in.

Courtney hopped out of the car and ran up to the steps.

"I don't think I'd go in there," Lois said, appearing at her side. "You could fall right through the floor."

"I have to go inside, Lois. I wonder if the steps around back are sturdier."

"Let's go see."

Courtney hurried around back, stepping over brambles, thistles, old lumber, rusty cans, and hubcaps. "Yes, these steps are better." She was up the steps in no time. It was imperative she at least look inside the house.

The rooms were bare except for dust, cobwebs, an old broken-down table, and stacks of newspapers. The late morning breeze blew through the broken-out windows. Then Courtney spied the staircase.

"The bedrooms are upstairs?"

"Yes. Your mother's was at the west end of the house." Lois took one look at the decaying steps and said she'd be outside. "I'm going to have a sneezing fit if I stay in here any longer. Be careful and walk on the outside of the steps."

"I'll just be a minute," Courtney replied.

Slowly, deliberately, she climbed the stairway, her hand clutching the railing. It was this stairway her mother had fallen from. Sadness welled up inside her. If only things could have been different.

Her mother's bedroom had tattered shreds for curtains hanging from one dingy window, the only one still intact. Courtney figured the bed would have been in the middle of the room. This was the room she'd been born in, the room her mother stayed in, slept in, dreamed in, and cried in. She'd also read here and wrote in a diary.

Courtney closed her eyes, saying a fervent prayer. "Lord, thank You for bringing me here. Thank You for letting me be in this room. And if my mother's in heaven, let her know I love her and wish I could have known her."

She took one more look before backing out of the room. If she came again, the house might be gone. She wondered why it hadn't already been torn down, but God knew of her need to see it, to walk up the steps to this room.

Lois was leaning against the car door, fanning herself. "You look like you've just seen a ghost."

"No—spirit," Courtney responded. "I've just been with my mother's spirit." She brushed damp hair back from the side of her face. "Thanks, Lois, for bringing me here. You have no idea what it means to me."

The older woman slipped an arm around Courtney's shoulder. "I'm glad you came to Darby."

"I am, too. I want to keep in touch," Courtney said. "I really do."

"And I with you."

"Perhaps you can come to Oregon sometime."

"Honey, people around here do not travel. I've never been farther west than the arch in St. Louis or farther east than Germantown."

"Oh. Then I will come here again."

"With your husband, I hope."

Courtney felt the fear again. "I don't know about that. He must be thoroughly disgusted with me. I returned the ring. He'll find someone else."

"Maybe not." Lois headed back to the car. "I'm betting he'll forget all that and be more than ready to give you the ring back."

Courtney wondered if he was worried about her, if he had flown back to Portland and gotten in touch with Alice. She hoped Alice wouldn't be upset. She owed her mother so much. Her life had been easy and filled with love and tenderness. How fortunate she was. She'd never realized just how much until now.

"I think you should call your—what did you say his name was?"

"Steven. Steven Spencer."

Lois smiled. "Courtney Cerise Spencer. It has a good ring to it, don't you think?"

"I'm still not sure about having a baby—"

"That's a decision you can make later."

"Later?" Courtney looked away. God was good. God had answered many prayers. He'd healed her that time eight years ago from the illness. He'd given her loving parents. He'd helped her locate her mother and her family. He'd brought Steven into her life. He'd given her a good job. She'd had her father's presence for the first twenty-one years of her life. Why couldn't she trust God with this one last thing, to give her a healthy child to love?

And then it hit her. What if the child wasn't healthy? Did that matter? She thought of a family at church who'd had a Down's syndrome child. Little Billy was the love of everyone. He was so loving and good-natured that people couldn't wait to see him, and when he had wanted to be an acolyte, Pastor Sam had agreed. "He will do a fine job," he said. And so he had. They just made sure his shoelaces were tied before going down the aisle, then Pastor suggested buying him shoes with Velcro.

Courtney looked over at Lois. "The fear I've felt is gone. I can't explain it, but suddenly I know that no matter what, I would love any child God gave me."

"Just as your mother loved you with all her heart and soul."

They drove back to Darby and sat and talked before ordering sandwiches back at the bakery. "I wish you the very best, Courtney," Lois said, "and by all means, call that young man of yours and apologize." She got into her car and waved as she backed out of the parking lot.

Courtney smiled, for she intended to do exactly that. On the seat beside her, a small box held all the treasures that would be dear to her the rest of her life. They would be passed down to her children and their children.

She wondered about Steven. What would she say? Would he forgive her? Or would he have given up and moved on with his life? She couldn't blame him if that was the case.

Pulling over, Courtney removed the cellular phone from her purse. Her fingers trembled as she started to dial the familiar number, but a tap on the window made her jump. She turned to look into the face of Melvin. He wasn't smiling.

twenty

Courtney was shocked to see Melvin. Had he been waiting for her? If so, why? Dressed in jeans, a clean white shirt, cowboy boots, and a rumpled hat, he motioned toward his truck. Courtney's heart tightened. *This might not be safe,* ran through her mind. What would she do if he suddenly drove off with her? She didn't like the dark, brooding eyes. Yesterday he had looked angry enough to hit her, and his disposition apparently hadn't changed.

"Hello," she finally said.

"I need to talk to you. Now."

He flung the passenger door open. She hesitated only a second. One didn't argue with a command like that. She prayed that it would be all right.

"I'm not sure if I—"

"What? Want to go with me?" He smiled. "Not much like your mother, I see."

"What do you mean by that?" *What did Melvin have to do with my mother?*

He helped her up into the high seat, closed the door, and hopped in beside her, but didn't turn the key.

"I have something to say and I ain't going to say it twice. What you do is up to you, of course."

"Does this concern my mother?"

"None other." He stared out the window, carefully avoiding her gaze.

"I'd known Vannah all my life. She was just there. One of the kids. Like the other girls. But she wasn't like the other girls." He paused, as if needing to catch his breath. "Not at all."

"What was she like?" Courtney reached over, touching his arm. "I want to know. I *need* to know."

He turned and scowled. "Why do you think I'm here?"

Courtney leaned back and sighed. "I have no earthly idea. All I know is that you seem to be angry with me—"

"Because people shouldn't go nosing around."

"You mean because I asked Lois about my mother? Because I am trying to find out who I am, you are holding that against me?"

"I know you mean well. Maybe I'd be doin' the same thing." He removed his hat and rubbed the top of his head. His hair was sparse and turning gray.

"You're not going to tell me—"

"I might if you'd stop interrupting. This ain't easy for me, believe me. Please hear me out. It'll only take a minute if you keep quiet."

Somehow Courtney wondered if this was going to be one of the longest speeches he'd ever made.

"I think your mother was one of the sweetest girls I'd ever known. I loved her and that's the God's truth."

"Loved her?"

He turned and scowled. "I asked youse not to interrupt."

"Sorry."

"I told my pa one night that I loved Vannah, and I thought he'd come unglued. Said I had to start thinking about more important things like farming and learning how to find a wife that'd be a help to me."

Courtney leaned back, the knot in her stomach growing tighter.

"I knew that Jon was no good for her. I tried to warn her, but she was in love with that guy, his car and all. Then, too, she saw him every day, working over in that big, fancy house. She didn't know how I felt about her because I couldn't tell her."

"When she turned up in the family way, she came to me, begged me to tell him. Well, I did, though I knew it wouldn't do one bit of good. His ma wouldn't let him marry her, just as my pa wouldn't let me even date her. Sure enough, I told Jon, but ol' rich boy wanted no part of it."

"And what did you do?" Courtney couldn't help it. She had to know.

"We never thought anyone would come a-looking. We heard that the baby had been adopted by an Air Force couple, and they were moving out of the area."

"Alice and Carl. My parents."

"Whatever." He still wouldn't look in Courtney's direction.

"But why come and tell me this now? You could have said it yesterday."

"Oh, no, I couldn't have."

"Why not?"

"Because Lois don't know."

"Lois doesn't know what?"

"That I loved Vannah with all my heart and soul. I never tol' her. Never intended to. What's the point? And I asked Lois to marry me a month after your mother died, but I never, ever forgot Vannah and I doubt I ever will. I should have stood up to Pa, taken her away, done something."

It was suddenly clear. Melvin had loved her mother. He'd wanted to marry her, wanted to raise another man's child. Was it because of this that he did not want children?

"I will never speak of this to Lois or anyone, I promise."

"Good. You can leave now. No need to talk to Lois anymore." He turned and made her look at him. "Do you want some money? I ain't got much, but there's some saved that

Lois don't know about."

Courtney couldn't believe he'd ask. Why would she take money from this man?

"I don't need money to keep me quiet."

"Here. I want you to have this." He pressed an envelope in her hand. "I've kept this all these years but want you to have it."

Courtney took the envelope and started to open it.

"No. Wait until I'm gone. Then look."

He hopped out of the truck, came to her side, and opened the door. "You know, you have her hair. Definitely. It's long and shiny, just like hers was. It really took me back when I saw you standing there in the front room."

Before she could answer, he jumped in behind the wheel, and the truck sped back down the highway toward home. Melvin could have been her father. He wasn't, but he'd loved her mother and just knowing that someone had loved her like that meant more than anything. Her hand touched her hair. Her mother's hair. She had her mother's hair.

She thought of Steven. If only she could talk to him now, feel his arm go around her protectively. If only. Her life seemed to be filled with if onlys right now.

Courtney went back to her car and got in. "Oh, God, thank You for letting me know this about my mother. And now, please help me to know what's right; give me some answers."

Her fingers clutched the envelope close, but she would wait to open it until after she called Steven.

twenty-one

Courtney had to work up the courage again to call Steven. Finally she dialed his cellular number and waited. He answered on the second ring, almost as if he had been waiting.

"Steven?"

"Courtney? Are you all right? Where are you? Can I come to see you?" His questions came out like bullets hitting a target.

"Courtney?" he repeated.

"I don't know where to begin," she finally answered, her fingers gripping the receiver hard.

"It doesn't matter. Can I come to be with you?"

"But you're too far away. I mean, you went back to Portland—"

"Wrong!"

"You didn't go back?"

"I'm in Belleville. I just couldn't leave, Courtney. I don't care if I lose the biggest contract in Portland. No way could I desert you now."

"I don't know what to say." Her heart thudded so loudly she was certain he could hear it over the wires.

"Say nothing unless it's 'I love you, Steven.' "

She laughed then. "That's the easiest part. Forgive me?"

"There's nothing to forgive. Now, where are you?"

"Back in Clancy."

"Sit tight. I'll be there. Should only take thirty minutes, forty-five tops."

Courtney decided to stay in the little park at the edge of town. Steven's voice had warmed her heart and her spirit. She didn't deserve him. She'd never deserved him. But, then, she didn't deserve to be God's child, either. But, thank goodness, her being saved did not rely on what she deserved.

With trembling fingers, she opened the small box Lois had so lovingly put together for her.

A few poems were on top. She read them with tears in her eyes. The first rhymed, and as Courtney read, she felt the grief her mother must have felt as a young, frightened girl.

A little baby I now carry
Though I can never marry
I pray she or he will always know
How much I cared, but could not show
O little child, I cannot keep
Surely you know how I weep
To another home you will go
But it was not my idea,
No, never my idea

Courtney could read no more. With tear-filled eyes, she laid the poems at the bottom and removed a small, leather-bound green book. *Five-Year Diary,* it said in gold letters.

Dare she open it? Could she bear to know what her mother's thoughts were? Her fears? She sat as afternoon sunlight poured through the window of the car. She prayed. She talked to her mother just as if she were in the car with her.

The diary was worn, the edges tattered. The writing was clear and written in a childish scrawl. Courtney's fingers touched the words. Precious words she would read. Soon she would know her mother and as she looked again at the faded snapshot of a laughing child in the middle, her heart tightened. Just one touch was all she'd ever wanted. But it wasn't to be. This had to be enough.

Papa has never understood me. He hates me. I'm only a burden and now I am bringing another burden into the world.

I can feel my baby move inside me. It's like magic. I put my hand on the bulge and it kicks back. I love my little baby so much.

Courtney shut the book. She couldn't read anymore. She took the small enevelope and carefully removed the purple ribbon. It was frayed on the edges as if it had been tied and untied many times.

A woven ring of white daisies dried to a fine powder was inside. Her mother had woven this bracelet of daisies for Mel? It had meant so much to him, he'd kept it all these years, yet knew how important it would be to Courtney, Vannah's child.

She wrapped it back and retied the ribbon. Such love he had felt and still felt. Could she feel that deeply toward Steven? Somehow she knew he cared for her in that wonderful way.

Courtney closed the diary. She'd read more later. She could only take so much at one sitting. "If only things had been different," she said out loud. "If only you had been allowed to keep me, Mama, but God in His infinite wisdom wanted me to belong to someone else. To bring love and laughter to a home. And, you, Mother, did that. If it weren't for you and your unselfish desire to give me to others, Alice and Carl would not have known such happiness.

"What you did was the ultimate sacrifice. Just as our God gave up His Son. None of us can know how that must have felt, not unless we were there."

A tap at the window made her jump. Steven's face loomed bigger than life as he motioned for her to unlock the door.

"Honey! Oh, honey." Then she was out of the car and into his arms. "I've been so worried. I couldn't sleep last night. Just kept praying I was doing the right thing. Then God gave me peace of mind. It was as if He was saying, 'My son, didn't I tell you to be patient? You must learn patience.' "

"Steven, I wouldn't blame you if you never wanted to see me again."

"Hush. I don't want to hear that." He lifted her chin, his mouth touching hers with a gentle kiss. "There. I just prayed I'd be able to hold you one more time, kiss you once more."

"I'm not afraid anymore, Steven." She raised her eyes to his. "It's all so wonderful. I can hardly wait to tell you."

"Shall we go somewhere or just sit in the car?"

"I feel more comfortable here."

"Okay." He came around to the passenger side.

An hour later, completely spent, Courtney leaned against Steven's shoulder, liking the feel of his arm around her, liking the smell of him, the words he'd spoken. It didn't matter that she hadn't known her father. It never had mattered.

"I haven't told you everything," Courtney said then.

"There's more?"

"Of course."

"Start in then."

She took a deep breath. "You know how worried I've been about having, well, you know, a family and all?"

"Yes."

"Lois told me that nobody ever has any guarantee, and God laid it on my heart that no matter what, you and I'd love our child, even if she or he were epileptic."

"Oh, honey, I've said that all along. Besides, there have been so many advances in medicine this past decade that our child would never suffer as your real mother did."

"Do you suppose I should call Mom and tell her we're on our way home?"

"Yes." Steven removed the box from his coat pocket. "But after this is back in place."

The stone shone as he slipped it back on her finger. "Here to stay this time, right?"

"Yes, Steven. Here to stay."

He lifted her face for a kiss. And then another.

"There's something we have to do before we leave."

"And that is?"

"You have to meet Dorcas. My paternal grandmother."

"Lead the way."

Dorcas invited them in and Courtney told her all that had happened. "I'll write you," she said. "I want to keep in touch."

They clung together and Dorcas handed her a small box. "It's just a few things I thought you might like for keep-sakes. A few photos of your father and a small quilt I made for him."

Courtney wiped away the tears gathering at the edge of her eyes. "Thank you so much. I love you." And they clung together again.

"You take good care of her for me," Dorcas said. "But I know you will. I'm just sorry for all that happened, my child. I hope you understand and can forgive me." Her eyes watered as she recalled how sick her son had been. "I couldn't bear to see him marry anyone at all. It was as if I knew he wouldn't live long here on Earth."

"It's over and done with," Courtney said. "I'm just glad I got to meet my real father's family."

She left with Dorcas in the doorway, waving.

And as the sun slipped behind a low layer of clouds, the couple held each other's hands while they skipped down the path toward the car.

epilogue

Mrs. Alice Adams and the late Carl Adams
request your presence at the marriage
of their daughter
Courtney Cerise Adams
to
Steven Andrew Spencer
Saturday evening
December 18, 1999
At half past seven at
Parkrose Community Church
Reception following in the church fellowship hall.
RSVP

"There. The last one is sealed and stamped," Courtney declared, "except this one that I must deliver in person."

"Gerta?" Alice looked puzzled. "Who is this, dear?"

"She's from the soup kitchen. You'll love her, Mom. She's a very sweet old lady and a good friend."

"Oh?" Her mother looked even more puzzled as she added her envelopes to the towering stack. "Any friend of yours is a friend of mine."

"The wedding of the year," Aunt Agnes said.

"And it will be. Yes, it will be." Courtney's eyes were shining.

"Mom, you sure you don't mind my changing my middle name legally to Cerise?"

"Of course not, darling. Now let's look at the beautiful wedding dress again."

"Gladly."

Alice removed it from the protective plastic bag. "It's just too beautiful."

Courtney held the full-length white taffeta gown to her cheek. The scoop neckline would show off the lovely necklace of pink Chinese sea pearls, a gift from Aunt Agnes. A double-tier veil, long white gloves, and dainty white satin slippers made the ensemble complete. White orchids and stephanotis made up the bridal bouquet. She'd seen a picture in a floral catalogue and knew that was what she wanted.

"If Dad were here, he'd make some comment such as, 'What a lovely gunnysack. Too bad they didn't have such things when your mother and I married.' "

"I miss him so much, Mom."

"I know, dear. So do I. But you can honor his memory by having the best marriage ever."

"I'm just glad I found some of my family," Courtney said.

Alice hugged her. "Yes, you finally *found* Courtney."

"Not that I was really lost."

"But you thought you were."

Courtney thought back to the six months when she was ill, how she'd asked God to spare her life because she had lots of living to do. "And I want to wear a white wedding dress and walk down the aisle and look longingly into the eyes of the man I will spend the rest of my life with," had been her prayer.

And God had granted that request.

A Letter To Our Readers

Dear Reader:

In order that we might better contribute to your reading enjoyment, we would appreciate your taking a few minutes to respond to the following questions. We welcome your comments and read each form and letter we receive. When completed, please return to the following:

Rebecca Germany, Fiction Editor
Heartsong Presents
PO Box 719
Uhrichsville, Ohio 44683

1. Did you enjoy reading *Finding Courtney?*
   - ❑ Very much. I would like to see more books by this author!
   - ❑ Moderately
   I would have enjoyed it more if ______________

   ____

   ____

2. Are you a member of **Heartsong Presents**? Yes ❑ No ❑
   If no, where did you purchase this book? ______________

   ____

3. How would you rate, on a scale from 1 (poor) to 5 (superior), the cover design? ______________________

4. On a scale from 1 (poor) to 10 (superior), please rate the following elements.

   _____ Heroine _____ Plot

   _____ Hero _____ Inspirational theme

   _____ Setting _____ Secondary characters

5. These characters were special because______________________

____

____

6. How has this book inspired your life?______________________

____

____

7. What settings would you like to see covered in future **Heartsong Presents** books?________________________

____

____

8. What are some inspirational themes you would like to see treated in future books?_________________________

____

____

9. Would you be interested in reading other **Heartsong Presents** titles? Yes ❑ No ❑

10. Please check your age range:

❑ Under 18 ❑ 18-24 ❑ 25-34

❑ 35-45 ❑ 46-55 ❑ Over 55

11. How many hours per week do you read?______________

Name ____

Occupation ____

Address ____

City _________________ State ___________ Zip ___________